YETTA'S YEARNING

The Alphabet Mail-Order Brides Book 24

MICHELE LINDSEY

Yetta's Yearning

The Alphabet Mail-order Brides Book 24

Michele Lindsey

Copyright 2019 by Michele Lindsey

All rights reserved.

No part of this book may be reproduced in any form or by any electronic or mechanical means, including information storage and retrieval systems, without written permission from the author, except for the use of brief quotations in a book review.

About the Series

For decades, The Wigg School and Foundling Home of New York City has been the home and education of many of the city's orphans. In fact, the current teachers are Madam Wigg's first "crop" of students, all grown into accomplished young ladies. But she is bothered by the idea of them spending the rest of their lives tied to the Home, without ever finding love. Madam Wigg knows each one of them dreams of being in charge of her own school, so she makes them all an offer…

Introduction

Now that his mine has paid out, Nathaniel can finally hang up his pickaxe and fulfill his dream of owning a cattle farm. He's also looking forward to settling down and starting a family. But he'll need a wife first.

Yetta has spent her whole life at the Wigg Foundling Home and School in New York City. First as a foundling herself, now as teacher, living in the dorms. Longing for adventure and yearning for a family of her own, she jumps at the chance to go west and start her own school. Turns out, becoming a mail-order bride is just the way to make it all happen.

It seems Yetta's found everything she was looking for – a loving husband, a community in need of a school, and adventure to last a lifetime. But will the excitement be too much and send her back to the safety of the Wigg School?

Chapter One

Yetta looked at the envelope in her hand one last time. Her breath caught in her chest, and her hand began to shake.

"Mr. Nathaniel E. Price, Colorado Springs, Colorado," she read quietly to herself. Up until this moment she'd been excited about the idea of picking her husband from an ad in a magazine.

"What's the matter?" Vera Mae asked, standing by her side.

Yetta looked at her with concern. "What if I didn't choose correctly? What if he isn't *the one*?"

"We're choosing grooms from a catalogue, Yetta. So chances are pretty slim that we'll find *the one*." Vera waved her hand and added, "Besides, I think that ideal is a bunch of hogwash only found in fairytales. I believe that we can grow to love any man who is kind and able to provide."

Yetta thought of the ad placed by Mr. Price. He'd mentioned he was "of moral character and able to provide a good life." While important, it was the words "seeking adventurous woman ready to start a family and willing to embrace homestead living" that called to her.

Yetta's Yearning

Yetta loved the other women at the Wigg School and Foundling Home, even thought of them as sisters. After all, they were foundlings themselves, who grew up at the orphanage. They'd known each other all their lives. And though they were grown, the women had stayed on with Madam Wigg and now taught at the school.

But Yetta craved more. She wanted out of the city. She longed for adventure. And she yearned for a family of her own.

"Next," the postmaster called, shaking her from her thoughts. She flashed a glance at Vera, who urged her on.

Yetta swallowed hard and stepped forward. Standing tall, she took a deep breath and extended her arm. *This is it.*

The postmaster slid the envelope from her fingers and gave it a quick glance. "Two cents."

Yetta scrounged two cents from her reticule and paid the man. This didn't leave her with much, reminding her again of why they were becoming mail-order brides.

It had all started a couple months ago, when Madam Wigg—or Wiggie as they called her—approached some of the older teachers with news that she was dying. Wanting her legacy to live on and her "girls" to spread their wings, she made a generous offer: go west, open a school, and she'd help fund it. That offer came with an interesting idea attached to it—a possible way for the women to pay for the travel and initial cost of starting the school: become mail-order brides.

The idea had sounded crazy at first, but as the rumors spread through the school and the women began perusing *The Bride's Bulletin*, the idea caught on like wildfire. There was just one problem, Wiggie thought Wendi, Vera Mae, Zara, and Yetta were too young to make such a move, so the offer was not extended to them. However, after a little begging and a lot of talk, Wiggie agreed with one condition: they must find a husband or no deal.

Yetta's nerves still had a hold on her when they stepped back out onto the street. But Vera wouldn't have it.

"Come on, don't be a wet blanket," Vera joked.

She hooked Yetta's arm and pulled her along as she started skipping cheerfully toward the school. After nearly half a city block, Yetta was giggling so hard she had to stop and catch her breath.

With a hand to her chest, Yetta said, "Thanks, I needed that. I don't know what's gotten into me."

They started for home again, this time at a casual pace.

"Things are changing," Vera said, putting an arm around Yetta's shoulder as they walked. "And I think everyone has been a little out of sorts because of it. But think of all the new and exciting things to come."

Yetta hugged her dear friend. "Some little town out there is going to be very lucky to have you as their teacher."

"And some wonderful man is going to be very lucky to have you as his wife," Vera returned.

———

NATHANIEL HEARD the wagon before he saw it. He knew it would be Simpson returning with another load of lumber. He put down his hammer and went to greet him, his Australian shepherd, Harley, on his heels.

"Whoa, whoa," Simpson said, pulling on the reins to slow the team.

"Good timing, I was down to my last few planks," Nathaniel said as the wagon pulled to a stop. He patted a horse as he walked toward the back of the wagon. His gaze rose to the dark clouds cresting the not-so-distant mountains. "Looks like we've got a storm rolling in."

Simpson wiped his brow and hopped down. "It sure would be nice to get a break from this heat." He followed Nathaniel to the back of the wagon and cast a glance over his shoulder. "I'd say we've got at least an hour. Maybe we can get this framing done before it hits."

"I sure hope so. We've had too many delays already." He hoisted a load onto his shoulder. "I can't, in good faith, go through with a marriage until I have more to offer than a half-finished home."

Clara, Simpson's wife, suddenly appeared next to the wagon. "You have plenty to offer a woman," she scoffed with her hands on her hips.

Nathaniel smiled. "You're sweet, but you're like a mother to me, so you have to say that."

"Oh, come now, you know that's not true," Clara said with a flick of her wrist. Then to her husband, she said, "Tell him, John." She was the only one who called him by his given name.

Simpson and his wife had been with the Price family since Nathaniel was a boy. Clara helped with the everyday household chores of the large homestead, and Simpson had worked alongside Nathaniel's father with their cattle business back in Texas.

As Nathaniel carried his load off, Clara turned her attention to her husband. "Did you pick up the things I needed from the mercantile?"

"Sure did; sack is on the bench." Then to Nathaniel he added, "Went to the post office too."

Suddenly woozy, Nathaniel lowered the planks to the ground and removed his hat. "Oh," was all he said.

"Ain't ya gonna ask?" Simpson prodded.

Nathaniel let out a sigh, scrubbed at his hair, and

replaced his hat. "Nope. Got too much work to do. It can wait until we break for supper."

It had been several days since they'd been to town, and the last time they'd checked, Nathaniel hadn't received a single response from his ad for a bride. But he knew Simpson well enough to realize that wasn't the case this time. While he was curious and somewhat anxious to see who'd responded, he was also a bit uneasy about his choice to place the ad in the first place.

"I left some fresh lemonade on the porch for you fellas," Clara said before grabbing the sack from the wagon and heading back toward the one-room house the three of them were currently living in.

Nathaniel had built the small house a few years after he first came to Colorado. He'd come—against his father's wishes—amidst the excitement of the gold rush seven years ago. His father, Theodore Price III, didn't understand Nathaniel's need to strike out on his own. He didn't see anything wrong with being a part of the family-run cattle empire. Sure, for some people, that was fine. But not so much for Nathaniel. He didn't want to spend a lifetime under the shadow of his father and two older brothers. Or ride the coattails of their success. He wanted to make his own way in the cattle business—the gold mining was just a means to an end.

About three months ago, Simpson and his wife had shown up on Nathaniel's doorstep, looking for work. It seemed loyalty meant nothing to Theodore. And after forty years of service, he'd put them out to pasture, hiring younger help.

Their timing was perfect, as Nathaniel's mine had recently paid out and he finally had the funds he needed to ready his land and purchase his first herd. Having Simpson there to lend his expertise and help in the work was proving invaluable. They'd already improved the barn and begun acquiring other livestock needed to run both the homestead and the business.

Now they were working on a home for Nathaniel to move into, so the three of them didn't have to live on top of each other.

After a quick lemonade break, Nathaniel and Simpson got to it. They worked hard to keep ahead of the looming storm, Nathaniel driving the nails into the wood as fast as Simpson could bring it to him. They managed to finish with no time to spare, the first crack of thunder oddly synchronizing with Nathaniel's last swing of his hammer.

He looked up to the sky as the thunder reverberated through the valley. Then he brought his gaze to the hammer in his hand and chuckled.

Simpson gave him a sideways glance.

"I am Thor, God of Thunder," Nathaniel quipped, brandishing his hammer and flexing his muscles.

Then, with unfortunate timing, thunder cracked again, and a bright flash of lightning immediately followed. Nathaniel startled and cowered, eyes to the sky, dropping his hammer in the process.

Simpson cackled. "Pick up your hammer, Thor, and let's get inside."

They quickly tossed their tools in the wagon. And while Nathaniel took off on foot, Simpson hopped into the front of the wagon.

The skies opened and released a torrent of rain. Nathaniel dipped his head against the downpour. Not only was it blinding, it was loud. He barely heard his own howls of protest as the icy droplets instantly chilled him to the bone.

Water splashed with each footfall, the rain coming too fast for the ground to drink it up. He got to the barn and whipped open the doors just in time for Simpson to pull the wagon in.

"Harley," he called, "come on, girl!"

The dog scooted inside, and Nathaniel closed the heavy barn doors behind them. Nathaniel turned his back as Harley began shaking dry, her ears slapping noisily as water sprayed every which way.

Simpson went about unhitching the wagon, while Nathaniel grabbed a couple blankets to wipe down the horses. "Golly! It's cold as a frog's behind," Nathaniel complained.

"I sure hope Clara's got the stove goin' by time we get in there," Simpson said.

With the horses dried and put away, Nathaniel grabbed a sheet of canvas he sometimes used to cover and secure cargo in the wagon bed and moved to the front of the barn. They didn't need to look outside to know the rain hadn't let up. But at this point they just wanted to get to the house and out of their sodden clothes.

The men stood beside one another and draped the canvas over their heads and shoulders, each taking hold of the thick material in hopes of shielding themselves, at least a little, from the torturous weather. The small house was a good hundred feet away.

Nathaniel cracked the door. "Ya ready?"

"As I'll ever be," Simpson answered.

After ordering Harley to stay, they stepped outside, secured the door behind them, and took off running. Nathaniel had to be sure not to go too fast so that Simpson could keep up.

The door opened the moment they stepped onto the porch, and Clara ushered them inside.

Simpson entered first, hugging himself and rubbing at his arms.

"Woo-eee!" Nathaniel hooted, shoulders raised and hands clenched at his sides. He kicked the door closed with the toe of his boot. The room was dark for three-thirty in the afternoon, even with the oil lamp on the mantle.

The men began stripping down to their underwear while Clara moved about gathering their laundry off the floor.

"Towels and blankets are on the table," she said. "And I got the stove fired up—will have some coffee for you soon."

A square table and four chairs sat in the middle of the room, between the door and the fireplace. To the left of the door was the kitchen space. And to the right, a small bedroom nook, currently occupied by Simpson and his wife. Nathaniel took up the space in the back-left corner of the main room, his bed shoved against the wall and a wooden trunk at the foot.

He looked forward to completing the work on his new, larger home. The one he'd share with his wife…as soon as he chose one.

And with that, he remembered that Simpson had gone to the post office.

"Where'd you put the letter?" he asked Clara, assuming she'd removed it from the sack along with her supplies.

"They're on the mantle."

One brow arched, his voice deepened. "They?"

"There are six."

"Well I'll be," he said, rubbing the stubble on his chin. He was beginning to think his advertisement had come off too pithy and rigid, leaving him undesirable. But the only advertising he'd ever done before was for business, where short and to the point was preferred.

He wrapped a blanket around his shoulders and crossed the room to retrieve his mail.

"I see you're limping," Clara said. "Leg bothering you again?"

"It's just the sudden change in the weather," Nathaniel answered as he settled in at the kitchen table.

"Want me to make you some tea with feverfew?" she said. "It'll help with the pain."

"No, thank you, Clara." As he worked the seal on an envelope, she came over and lit the lamp on the table. She was always looking out for him.

Nathaniel read the first letter. It was from a thirty-four-year-old woman with three kids. He was a bit disappointed. He didn't want an older woman who already had a family.

He moved on to the next letter. It was from a seventeen year old who lived with her father in an apartment above his shop. Most of the letter was spent complaining about having to work. Nathaniel's disappointment grew. *She sounds spoiled and lazy*, he thought as he shoved the letter back into the envelope.

He sat back in his chair and sighed.

Simpson sat across from him at the table. "That bad, huh?"

"This may be harder than I thought."

Clara approached the table. She held two cups by the handles in one hand and a kettle in the other.

The smell of fresh coffee teased Nathaniel's nose. But if the rest of these letters were as bad as the first two, he'd need something stronger than coffee.

"You're talking about choosing a wife. Someone who'll bear your children," Clara said as she began pouring. Then, quite gruffly, she added, "Not hiring a ranch hand."

Clara was right. He was looking for someone to spend the rest of his life with. He wanted a marriage with love. This was not something to be rushed. He reminded himself that he didn't even have to choose from these first responses, at least not right away.

Nathaniel took a few minutes to relax and sip his coffee before continuing with a new frame of mind.

The next three letters he read gave him more hope. Any one of those women, it seemed, would make a fine wife. But it was when he read the last letter that he knew he'd found *the one*.

Dear Mr. Price,

I am interested in becoming your bride. I saw your advertisement in The Bride's Bulletin, and while you offered few details about yourself and what you have to offer, it was the word "adventurous" that caught my attention. So, with that in mind, I will tell you a little about myself and leave it for you to decide if you'd like to correspond further.

I am a teacher at a foundling school in New York City, the one in which I grew up. While I enjoy teaching, I dream of getting out of the city and having a family of my own. I want to see grass and mountains and know what it's like to breathe fresh air. I love animals and hope one day to see something more exciting than a city rat. The idea of living on a homestead excites me. I am a hard worker.

As to my looks, I would say that I am reasonably good looking. I am of average size and height. I have long, honey blond hair and hazel eyes.

While I realize that choosing a spouse in this manner seems more like a business deal, I would like to add that I do not want a loveless marriage. If this is not something you can offer, then I ask kindly that you disregard this letter, and I wish you well in your endeavors.

Hope to hear from you.
Sincerely yours,
Yetta Wigg

Chapter Two

Yetta closed the door quietly behind her, careful not to wake the children. It had taken Cindy longer than usual to fall asleep tonight. The poor child had lived a horribly abusive life before she came to the orphanage a few months ago. Nighttime was hard for Cindy, so Yetta always sat with her until she fell asleep.

As Yetta made her way through the dimly lit corridors, the anticipation grew. Waiting for her in her room was a letter from Mr. Price. All day she'd been waiting for the opportunity to read it. And now, while most everyone slept, was her chance.

She yawned as she opened the door and slid into the room she shared with Zara. Their room was small, like most of the teachers' rooms. It had two beds shoved into the corners, separated by a bedside table. A small chest of drawers sat near the door.

Zara was used to Yetta coming in late and had left their bedside lamp burning for her. It was a hot summer night in the city; noise from the street flowed in through the open window.

After changing into her nightclothes, she retrieved the letter from between the pages of the book on the bedside table and climbed into bed.

She was surprised at how nervous she was—almost to the point of feeling nauseous. For the past several weeks, the other women had been hearing from their grooms and sharing their excitement. A few had even left the school already.

Abigail had been the first to go. She had two young children and found a nice man who was looking for an instant family. From her letters, it seemed she was quite happy, and her children Joshua and Maggie were thriving.

Yetta missed Maggie dearly; the five year old had a love for animals, just like herself. They often had fun outside, enjoying what little nature could be found on the busy streets of New York City.

As Yetta carefully opened the seal on the envelope, she wondered if it was finally her turn.

She took a deep breath as she unfolded the letter. It was two pages, and tucked inside the folds, she found a train ticket and money. Both a good sign. She stuffed them back into the envelope for safe keeping and started reading.

DEAR MISS WIGG,
I was delighted to read your response…

A SCREAM YANKED Yetta from the bed. She was across the room in two steps, yanking open her bedroom door.

Bang! Boom!

It was coming from Emmeline and Dorthy's room down the hall.

Without hesitation, Yetta rushed toward the commotion. Weary eyes peeked through slightly-cracked doors as she passed.

As Yetta reached their room, she heard another scream and burst through the door.

Emmeline stood on top of her bed, pressing herself into the corner. "Get it, Yetta!" She pointed toward a rat walking along the floorboard.

Dorthy watched from her bed, a grimace on her face.

Yetta rolled her eyes. She scooped the rat and held it up, admiring its pink nose and fluffy whiskers. "Is this cute little thing what all that excitement was about?" She laughed and extended her arms toward Emmeline in a devilish sister kind of way.

Emmeline's nose wrinkled; she tried to climb higher up the wall. "Ewww! Get it away!"

"Yetta," a voice said sternly behind her. It was Wendi.

Yetta pulled the rat in close and turned, pressing her lips. "Sorry, Wendi."

"It's not me you need to be apologizing to."

Yetta glanced sheepishly over her shoulder. "Sorry, Emmeline."

The woman climbed down off the bed. Her brow knitted, she shrugged and let out a you-got-in-trouble sort of moan.

"Aaand," Wendi prodded.

"Thank you for capturing the disgusting rodent," Emmeline conceded. "Now if you'd kindly remove it from my room…"

Many of the other women had gathered in the hall. They gave Yetta plenty of room as she made her way through the crowd.

Once outside, she bent and carefully released the rat near the street gutter. It paused, sitting up to look at her.

"Sorry, little fellow, but you don't belong inside." She stood and waved her hand. "Go on, now."

The rat disappeared into a storm drain, and Yetta turned toward the building. Wendi was watching from the open door.

"Ooh, Yetta," she sighed with a look of endearment as Yetta approached. "You are going to give some poor groom a run for his money, aren't you?" She ended with a laugh.

Yetta felt herself blush. Then she remembered the letter waiting for her back in the room. She tried to hide a smile.

Wendi cocked a brow. "Well, don't you look like the cat who ate the canary." Her eyes widened as though she'd just realized why. "Did you hear from your groom?" she squealed in delight.

"Shhhh!" Yetta giggled.

Wendi joined her, giggling quietly as to not disturb the other women again. She draped her arm over Yetta's shoulder and led her back toward their rooms. "Well? What did he say?"

"I don't know yet," Yetta answered. "I was just about to read his letter when Emmeline started making a fuss. But…" she teased with a smile.

"But, what?" Wendi's voice edged louder again.

"He did send a train ticket and money for travel expenses," Yetta said.

"Oh my! You must be absolutely dying!"

Yetta nodded vehemently as they stopped in front of her door.

"I'm so happy for you," Wendi said, hugging her friend before scampering off to bed.

Yetta slid quietly into her room once again. Zara was awake this time, sitting on the edge of her bed.

"What was all the noise about?" Zara asked.

"Oh, nothing." Yetta waved it off, too eager to get back to Mr. Price's response.

She looked down at the letter on her bed and gasped. There was only one page—the second one. In all the excitement, what had happened to the first page?

Yetta frantically pulled at the bedding.

"What's wrong?" Zara asked.

"Did you see another piece of paper?" Yetta's pulse raced as panic set in.

"No." Zara stood, sweeping her eyes over the dimly lit room.

Yetta got down on her knees and checked under her bed.

"Wait, what's this?" Zara asked as she bent to grab it.

The next sound Yetta heard was…

Rip!

Yetta let out a gasp.

So did Zara.

"I'm sorry." Zara grimaced, handing the page to Yetta. It was missing part of the bottom right corner. "I didn't realize it was wedged under the leg of my bed."

"That's all right. I know it was an accident."

Yetta checked the last few words on the page; the sentence continued to the second. Relief washed over Yetta. She smiled. "It doesn't look as though anything is missing."

Dear Miss Wigg,

I was delighted to read your response to my advertisement! We may be kindred spirits as I too have a propensity for adventure. I am originally from Texas but came to Colorado about seven years ago to get in on the excitement of the Pike's Peak gold rush. It has proven to be quite profitable and allowed me the funds needed to get into the cattle business.

I have built a good life here in Colorado and as my bride, I can ensure you will want for nothing. I am in the process of finishing construction on a larger home for us on Triple Peak Ranch. The smaller, original home will go to my live-in help and give us the privacy a newly-wed couple will want. I think you'll love John "Simpson" and his wife, Clara. They are like family to me.

Between the daily chores on the ranch and working on our home, I expect to be quite busy until the moment you arrive. The ride from town is just under a half hour. I will…

…PICK you up from the train station. Clara will have dinner ready for your arrival as I'm sure you'll be hungry and eager to rest after your long journey.

I'd like to get married sooner rather than later but want you to be comfortable. If you would prefer to wait a week or two, we can discuss. I have enclosed a train ticket and ample funds to cover any further travel expenses. Please use however you see fit. I hope I have given you enough time to tie up all loose ends before you travel west.

UNTIL THEN,
I remain your humble servant and now betrothed,
Nathaniel E. Price

THE NIGHT AIR was cold and crisp, not a cloud in the sky. Nathaniel lay on his bedroll in front of the crackling fire, his back resting against a large rock, a cup of warm beans in his hand, and his beloved shepherd by his side.

"This is the life," he said with a smile, looking over to Simpson.

"You did it, kid," Simpson replied. "Triple Peak is officially in business."

They'd met up with Charles Landing along the Goodnight-Loving Trail early in the day to purchase one thousand head of cattle. Moving the longhorns from the trail to Triple Peak was a two-day drive. They expected to arrive well before sunset tomorrow, as long as they didn't run into any trouble.

Being back in the saddle, driving cattle, felt right to Nathaniel. And he had a good team with him. Simpson, of course, along with two highly recommended hired cowhands, and his new full-time ranch hand Jacob. He was a boy of seventeen who was quite happy to have the work and to bed in Nathaniel's barn.

"It's hard t' believe that this time next week, you could be a married man," Simpson said.

Thoughtfully, Nathaniel reached over and rested his free hand on Harley's back. It *was* hard to believe. It seemed like suddenly everything he ever wanted would be his.

The dog lifted her head to meet his eyes; Nathaniel patted her. "I just hope she can love me as much as you do, girl," he said, and she lowered her head again.

Chapter Three

Yetta popped her head in the room to check on Wendi. "I can't believe we're leaving the school tomorrow." The feeling was bittersweet.

"I know. It seemed to happen so fast," Wendi said as she checked her bag.

Yetta's eyes moved across the room, past Vera's bed, to the empty corner that once held a third bed. Xenia's. After being empty for a while, it had been decided that the bed was needed elsewhere. Wendi and Vera had fought it; they'd still been hopeful that Xenia would return one day. Even though they'd both feared—deep down—that she was dead. After all, she'd disappeared without a trace.

Wendi caught Yetta staring. "We may never know," she said mournfully. Wendi carried a guilt and obligation for Xenia that no one could convince otherwise. Not that they didn't try.

"It's no one's fault, Wendi," Yetta said. "You have to believe that."

Everyone had their own theory of what had happened to Xenia. The girl was passionate and headstrong, and she believed that she could somehow fix the world. And while some felt that's what led to her demise, Yetta believed she was out there, doing just that. Fixing the world. One criminal at a time, probably working undercover for the Pinkerton Detective Agency.

Yetta's mouth curled at the thought. Yes. She had to believe her friend was a hero.

Taking a deep breath, Yetta pulled herself from her thoughts and plunked down on Vera's bed. "Are you sure you have everything?"

"It's not like I'm taking much." Wendi sat beside her bag on the bed opposite and smiled. "None of us are."

"That's true, but we have what we need." Yetta looked down at her hands in her lap and flicked her nails together. Her gaze rose to meet Wendi's. "Do you think you'll love him?" she asked in earnest.

"I'm not doing this to fall in love," Wendi said practically as she twirled a lock of her long reddish-brown hair. "This is about the children. From what Mr. Bennet wrote, I think they are in need of a teacher who can help them develop and grow. All children should learn to learn."

"Yes, I know," Yetta said, rolling her eyes. She'd heard Wendi's philosophy a dozen times. Verbatim, she repeated, "Your goal is to instill a lifelong love of learning in every child."

"That's right," Wendi said, lifting her chin. "Every child should have the opportunity to learn, but they need to learn *how* to learn first..." Her voice trailed off as Yetta's mind wandered.

When Wendi finished, Yetta said, in a somewhat joking manner, "I just hope your Mr. Bennet has the same ideas, or life married to you is not going to be easy."

Wendi stood. "We have to stick to what we believe. You'll remember that, won't you?"

"You know I will," Yetta said, giving her friend a hug.

As the girls parted, the door opened, and Vera walked in. "What are you two doing standing around chatting? You know we have to be at the train in the morning."

Wendi and Yetta smiled at each other and chimed, "We know."

The three of them, along with Zara, would be traveling together, and Vera was compulsive about this sort of thing. With Vera, everything had to be just right. Even now, her blonde hair was perfectly coiffed and her blue dress immaculate.

THE NEXT MORNING, while the porter loaded their trunks onto the train, the women said goodbye to their loved ones who'd come to see them off. It was a mixture of tears and laughter. And lots of promises to keep in touch.

Then it was time to say goodbye to Wiggie.

"I packed up enough food to last you all a few days," Madam Wigg said, holding up a hamper. "Sandwiches, apples, and a few other things." She set it on the ground beside the women's smaller bags they'd carry on themselves.

"Thank you," the women chimed.

"I'm going to miss you, Wiggie," Vera said, rushing in for a hug.

The two exchanged a few final words. Then Vera stepped away, wiping tears from her eyes with the back of her hand.

Wendi went in for a hug next. After a few quiet words between them, they parted.

"You stay true to yourself, Wendalynn," Madam Wigg said.

Wendi sniffled and nodded.

Tears traced lines down Yetta's cheeks. It was her turn.

"Thank you for everything," she cried into Wiggie's neck.

Wiggie squeezed tighter and whispered in Yetta's ear. "Go have a wonderful life, my dear."

Yetta stepped back, wiping her tears with a handkerchief. She nodded, assuring Wiggie that's what she intended to do.

Madam Wigg turned her attention to Zara. She opened her arms wide, inviting her in. "And my Zara. Always last, but *never* least." She smiled.

The train whistle blew, indicating it was time to board.

A few minutes later, the women took their seats on the train. They were lucky to find four together on one side of the aisle, two would ride backwards facing the other two.

They were barely settled when train started to pull away. The women leaned toward the windows and waved goodbye to Wiggie. She waved back, watching them with a gentle smile on her face, as the train left the station.

Yetta continued to watch until she could no longer see Wiggie. And as the train moved away from the parts of the city that were familiar, she was overwhelmed with the reality that she was truly leaving her old life behind. The anticipation of what lay ahead made her reach for Zara's hand. She was grateful to have her sisters with her. At least for the first couple of days. They'd say goodbye to Zara first, as she'd change routes toward Montana. Then they'd lose Wendi in Nebraska. And turned out Vera and Yetta would be about a day's ride from each other in Colorado.

BY THE SECOND day on the train, the novelty had worn off, and the women were already tiring of their packed sandwiches. So they gladly shared with a mother traveling alone with her two young children; she too was headed west to be a mail-order bride.

Meeting the Bolt family was just what they needed to stave off boredom. The women enjoyed sharing her company, expressing their hopes and dreams for the future, and of course, the nervousness of it all. And Mrs. Bolt was grateful to have help with her little ones on the long journey. Between the four foundling sisters, the young mother got a few moments of peace and a chance to stretch her legs every so often. And of course, Zara never could resist sharing her beloved Greek stories and myths with children.

After several days on the train and saying goodbye to one friend after another, including friends she'd met along the way, it was down to Yetta and Vera Mae. They went all the way to Denver together. For Yetta, *this* was the longest goodbye. Her last connection to her old life. With tears streaming down her face, she held on tight.

The whistle blew, and the conductor called his final warning.

"All aboard!"

"You're going to miss your train," Vera said as she pried herself from Yetta's arms. "I promise I'll write as soon as I can."

Yetta nodded. "Me too," she said, sniffling.

She took a seat by the window and looked out at Vera, standing on the platform. As the train pulled away, she gave a final wave. She couldn't believe that in just a couple hours she would finally be at her destination.

Alone with her thoughts, the sound of the locomotive echoed louder than ever.

Clickety-clack! Clickety-clack! Clickety-clack!

The whistle blew as the train slowed, nearing the Colorado Springs station. Yetta pulled her braid toward the front and straightened her hat one last time. Primped and ready, her hands worried in her lap. From her window seat, she inspected every man who waited on the platform, wondering which one was her groom.

The brakes squealed, bringing the train to a stop. Yetta placed a hand on her carpet bag beside her to keep it from tumbling to the floor as the train lurched forward. Then with her reticule hanging from the crook of her arm, she grabbed the handle of the bag with two hands and hoisted it off the seat.

By the time Yetta exited the train, many of the people waiting on the platform had already claimed their passengers. Since she didn't know what Mr. Price looked like, she decided to let him find her. So she moved down to the luggage car and handed the porter her claim ticket.

She dropped her heavy bag at her feet and waited, glancing curiously at the dwindling crowd on the platform.

"Here ya go, miss," the porter said as he delivered her trunk.

"Thank you."

Now that she had her belongings, she was ready to go. The thought of Mr. Price not showing crossed her mind, sending her nerves on edge.

Yetta smoothed the hem of her suit jacket over her skirts with gloved hands. Vera's sweet voice played in her head, reminding her to check her posture. With her toes slightly outward, Yetta brought her heels together. She straightened her back and stood tall, then placed her hands together, palms facing, and fingers curled into each other.

She felt ridiculous, standing stiff and perfectly still as if she were on display.

Good heavens, it's hot.

A handsome gentleman caught her attention from one end of the platform. He seemed to be smiling at her. Yetta smiled back. He was walking toward her. And the closer he got, the harder her heart pounded. He was tall, dark, and...

He walked right on by, into another woman's arms.

Yetta tried to hide her embarrassment. She could only hope no one had noticed her excitement. And subsequent disappointment. Her mind was a flurry of thoughts and scenarios as she dug in her reticule for a fan. It was so busy, in fact, that she didn't notice the gentleman approaching, until he was standing right in front of her.

"Miss Wigg, I presume?"

"Yes," she answered in a rush. Her knees wobbled, and suddenly she was seeing two gentlemen standing in front of her.

"Are you all right?" he asked.

"I'm think I'm just a little—" she began, before everything went black.

THE RHYTHMIC VIBRATION soothed Yetta as she slept. She felt like she'd never get off this train. But then suddenly something didn't feel right. Gone was the smell of smoke and coal and the clacking sound of metal on metal.

Yetta's eyes blinked open. Bright blue sky passed above her, and she heard the steady cadence of hooves clipping and scuffing on a dirt-packed road.

Startled, she sat up bolt straight and saw the town of Colorado Springs disappearing in the distance.

Yetta was sitting in the back of a wagon, alongside her trunk.

"You're awake," the man driving the wagon said, glancing over his shoulder at her. "Would you like to join me up here?"

Yetta buried her face in her hands. What a disaster. This was not how she had visualized meeting her intended.

To make matters worse, when she looked up from her hands, she noticed her white gloves came away soiled.

"Want some water?" He reached back, holding a canteen.

Her eyes met his, and she finally got a good look at him this time. He wasn't necessarily a bad looking man. It was just that…well, to be honest, he looked much older than she'd imagined. The wrinkles at the corners of his eyes met with the heavily graying hair that peeked from beneath his hat. His skin had a leathery look, like he'd spent his whole life out on the range.

Yetta took the canteen, unscrewed the cap, and guzzled the warm water. She'd never been so thirsty. Water dripped down her chin when she pulled it from her lips and took a deep breath.

"Thank you," she said as she replaced the cap. Plucking a handkerchief from her sleeve, Yetta wiped her mouth and then the sweat and dust from her brow.

I must look atrocious, she thought as she reached into her carpet bag to retrieve her mirror.

He glanced back again, noticing her getting into her bag. "What you got in there, anyways? 'Tis heavier than a goat with no legs." He spoke with a bit of a nasally Texas drawl.

That strange image popped into her head. Her brow pinched. "Are legless goats particularly heavy?" she asked politely.

He cocked his head, then broke out in a belly laugh. "It's just a sayin'. A joke, really."

Yetta didn't understand.

"If you had a goat with no legs, you'd hafta carry it," he explained. Then he explained some more, "There ain't actually any legless goats."

"Oh." Feeling stupid, Yetta held the handkerchief to

her face and laughed. She remembered his original question. "I brought a few books—that's why the bag is heavy."

"Oh, right," he said, turning his attention back to the road in front of him. "The teacher thing," he added with an air of dismissal.

Yetta felt a knot in her chest. Did he have a problem with her being a teacher?

When she finally caught sight of her reflection, it confirmed the worst. Her face was dirty, her hair disheveled, and her hat gone from her head. She hadn't noticed it sitting beside her bag.

Yetta did her best to make herself presentable. She pinned her hair into a low bun and hid the rest of her hair under her hat. As she dusted off her clothes, she was pleased with herself for having the forethought to wear her camel-colored skirt and jacket for the long trip. It hid the dirt well.

Taking a deep breath, Yetta moved carefully—and nervously—to the front of the wagon. Then with as much grace as possible while in a long skirt, in a moving wagon, she climbed over the seat back of a bench. Her rump landed on the hard wood with a thud.

He looked over and smiled. His teeth were decent. At least it looked like they were all there.

"Not too much longer," he said. "You must be pretty tired of traveling by now."

In her mind, he meant she looked tired and hideous. She rolled her bottom lip in between her teeth to keep it from quivering. Then she silently criticized herself for setting her heart up for disappointment. For every time she had pictured meeting him, he'd commented on her beauty and they had fallen instantly and madly in love.

With a closed-lipped smile, she nodded politely. "Yes, I look forward to getting a bath and a restful night's sleep."

They rode the rest of the way in silence. Yetta focused on the beauty of the green, grassy hills and the magnificent Rocky Mountains beyond as they traveled north, alongside the mountain range. She made notice that, while people in the city lived on top of one another, out here it seemed the nearest neighbors were miles apart.

Eventually the wagon turned, so the mountains were ahead of them, growing closer and closer. Yetta wondered how much longer.

Then, as they approached the top of a knoll, he announced their arrival. "Welcome to Triple Peak." A moment later, she saw the sprawling homestead in the valley below, though it would be several minutes before they'd actually arrive.

Yetta couldn't help but smile. The place was impressive. The fact that this was going to be her new home seemed unreal. They passed wood rail fences on the left, behind which she spotted three horses grazing. Up ahead, a large barn sat to the left and what looked to be the main house to the right, with a small cabin tucked back between the two. Though very different, both homes looked inviting. One, simple yet cozy. The other was a two-story home with a wrap-around porch, complete with rockers.

Yetta glimpsed the man next to her again and sighed. *Maybe he's not so bad.*

The wagon slowed to a stop in front of the main house, and he hopped down.

Yetta considered waiting for his help, but she wasn't sure she was ready for his hands to be on her. So she stood and backed her way out of the wagon, using the side step.

The ground was further away than she thought. With pointed toe, she stretched and reached. And just when she was about to let go and hope for the best, two hands grabbed her by the waist.

"I've got ya." The voice was low and seductive, like velvet.

Once on solid ground, she peered over her shoulder. Her breath caught in her chest and her body spun in his arms.

Who was this man holding her so intimately?

Her hands moved to his rock-hard biceps. While her first thought was to put some distance between them, she found herself holding him in place. His nearly black hair fell forward in thick waves over his forehead as he looked down and gazed into her eyes. His were slate gray.

"Ahem." A throaty cough suddenly got their attention. "Prolly too late for introductions as it seems yer already gettin' to know each other, but…Miss Yetta Wigg, this is Nathaniel Price."

Chapter Four

Yetta's gaze met Nathaniel's again. Her mouth gaped. Then she busted out laughing, her body shaking in his arms. He wasn't sure what to think. He stepped back, smiling. But her adorable laugh was contagious, and soon he was laughing too.

As she attempted to pull herself together, she reached for her handkerchief and wiped the tears from her eyes. "*You're* Nathaniel Price?" Her cheeks were bright red.

"Yes."

"Then who is that?" She pointed to the other man who had gone to the back of the wagon to unload.

"That's Simpson," he answered with knitted brow. "In my letter I mentioned that I'd be sending him to meet you at the train."

"No." Yetta flashed a skeptical look as she retrieved the folded letter from her reticule. "I read your letter several times, and you most certainly did not say that you were sending Simpson."

She scanned the pages quickly and handed them to Nathaniel.

Nathaniel held a page in each hand. He skimmed the first and moved to the second. In an instant he realized why the confusion. He slid the pages back together in one hand and flipped up the torn corner.

"What happened here?" he asked.

"Long story, but it got stuck under a piece of furniture," she answered, her mouth pulling into a straight line.

He read the last bit of the page out loud. "The ride from town is just under a half hour. I will…" He looked up and smiled, then filled in the missing words from where the tear was. "Send Simpson to," he said, then picked up from the top of the next page, "pick you up from the train station."

Nathaniel paused, then addressed Simpson, "But didn't you introduce yourself?"

"I was gonna, but it got a little…complicated," he answered.

Yetta groaned and hid behind her hand.

Simpson quietly mimed that the woman had fainted.

Nathaniel nodded in understanding.

"No harm done," he said to Yetta. Then with an outstretched arm, he gestured toward the main house. "I bet you would like to get inside and freshen up from your travels."

"I would like that very much." She peeked at him from under the rim of her hat, her cheeks still rosy. Her gaze shifted away. "Now, if only soap and water could wash away my humiliation as well."

Nathaniel chuckled. He could tell the young woman was sprightly, that she was going to liven up the place.

As they approached the front porch, Yetta said, "Your home looks beautiful."

"Our home," Nathaniel corrected. "She's got good bones, but she's going to need your woman's touch." Her lips curled into a bashful smile. He could tell she was pleased. "I had Clara make up a room for you. I hope you'll find it to your liking."

"I'm sure it will be lovely, thank you."

The front door opened, and Clara greeted them with a smile, then headed straight for Yetta with arms open. "Welcome home, my dear."

"Miss Yetta Wigg, this is Clara," Nathaniel said quickly, before the woman swallowed her up in one of her legendary hugs. "She's very excited to have another woman around at last."

YETTA MELTED into the older woman's embrace. It reminded her of Madam Wigg; she always gave the best hugs. A twinge of sadness came over her. Saying goodbye to Wiggie—the only mother she'd ever known—had been one of the hardest things she'd ever done. Especially knowing that Wiggie was sick and…well, Yetta didn't want to think about that. At least she found some relief in that there was a chance of seeing a few of her foundling sisters again as several may have been living within a day's ride.

Releasing Yetta, Clara held her at arm's length. "Well, aren't you a cute little thing?"

Yetta blushed. "Thank you." While the compliment was nice, she was tired of always being referred to as cute or little, and worst of all…young. But that's what happened when you had so many older sisters. She only hoped Nathaniel would see her in a more *womanly* manner.

The moment the older man stepped through the door with Yetta's carpet bag, Clara began dealing out orders. "Could you fellas please take her things up to her room? And there's a pot of water on the stove for her to use to wash up."

Yetta's Yearning

Clara wrapped an arm around Yetta's shoulders. "Come, my dear, let me show you around." The fact that Clara called Yetta "my dear" warmed her heart, as it was a term Wiggie often used.

Off the center hall, to the right, was a cozy parlor with a settee and a sofa situated in front of a fireplace. A rocker sat off to one side; beside it was a table and lamp. At the other end of the room there was a small desk and a shelf of books. Yetta was happy to see books in the house. She looked forward to adding hers to the collection.

To the left of the center hall was the dining room. It also had a fireplace, as well as a sideboard and a table that would seat eight comfortably. In the right corner, there was a door that led into the kitchen.

The kitchen had a small table and looked well stocked. Clara had something in the oven and was in various stages of preparing dinner. They passed through and exited through a different doorway back to the center hall. They made their way up the stairs, Yetta following as Clara led the way.

"There are four bedrooms," Clara said as they reached the second floor. "Nathaniel's is the room on the right." She turned to Yetta with a pointed look, as if she'd said the wrong thing. "Oh, I guess I should call it the *master bedroom* since you'll be sharing it after the wedding."

"Sharing," Yetta repeated and swallowed hard. "Yes. Of course. Because that's what married people do."

The door was open. Yetta's eyes went straight to the bed, which sat opposite the door. It was so much bigger than the beds they'd had at the school. And fancy too, with a tall, ornate headboard made of solid wood. This was a bed for a married couple. Suddenly it all seemed so real.

Clara put a hand on Yetta's arm and spoke earnestly, "It's natural for a woman to be nervous."

Yetta's eyes flicked to the floor and back again.

"I thought maybe you'd be more comfortable if I stayed in the room down the hall, at least for tonight."

"I appreciate it." Yetta nodded. "Thank you."

"Of course." Clara paused with a smile, then continued her tour of the upstairs. "There are two rooms on the left. We've got you set up in this front room. I think you'll like it; it faces east. I love waking up to the mornin' sun, don't you?"

"Hmm. I'm not sure." Yetta couldn't recall ever waking up to the morning sun.

Surprise showed on Clara's face.

"I guess it's not a luxury we got in the city, being surrounded by large buildings and all."

"Well then, I'm glad I set you up in here. The sunrises are just breathtaking here." Clara stepped into the room and Yetta followed. She noticed her trunk had already been delivered, placed at the foot of the bed.

The room was elegant, done in robin's-egg blue and a dull yellow. And while it was large enough for two beds, it held only one. Again, the bed was arranged on the wall opposite the door. A chest of drawers sat to the right of the bed and a beautiful wash stand, complete with mirror on the wall adjacent. To the left of the bed was a side table adorned with a bouquet of fresh, wild flowers—a welcoming touch—and a small rocking chair in the corner. All the wood in the room matched, likely an entire bedroom set purchased from a catalog.

Yetta went to the window and peered out. She couldn't believe the view. Back in New York City, the view from her bedroom window was the side of the building next door. But here, she could see the fenced pasture they had driven past on the way in, and beyond that, just miles of beautiful Colorado landscape.

Yetta's Yearning

"Where would you like your bag, Miss Wigg?" Simpson asked.

Yetta turned from the window. "Anywhere is fine, thank you."

He placed the bag on top of the trunk. "You ladies need anything else before I go unhitch the wagon?"

Yetta shook her head. "No. But thank you again for all your help."

Simpson removed his hat, held it to his chest and gave a small bow. "My pleasure."

Yetta smiled. Now that she knew the older man wasn't her betrothed, she looked at him with a fresh pair of eyes. He was a kind man. Someone she *could* love, but in a fatherly way.

Clara relieved her husband with a simple nod. That fascinated Yetta. To be married to someone so long—to know someone so well—that words weren't needed. Would she and Nathaniel be like that someday? She could only hope.

As Yetta watched Simpson disappear around the corner, she had Nathaniel on her mind. He had to be the most ruggedly handsome man she'd ever laid eyes on. She wrapped her arms around herself remembering what it had been like when she was in his.

Suddenly Nathaniel stepped into view, jarring her from her daydream.

"Pardon the intrusion. Everything okay?" He held the wire handle of a large, cast-iron pot.

"Oh, yes, come in." Yetta rubbed the back of her neck. It was warm and tingly. "I'm just a little tired from all the traveling."

Nathaniel entered, crossing to the wash stand. He poured the warm water into the white porcelain pitcher sitting in the basin.

Yetta watched his every move. He was so different from men in the city. She was used to seeing lean businessmen in wool suits or clerks in aprons. But Nathaniel wasn't. Nor was he plump. He had broad shoulders and thick arms, decidedly from heavy work. And instead of wools of blacks or grays, he wore tan denim trousers.

He placed the pot on the floor and turned. "I'll leave this here in case you need more."

She gave a slight nod. "Much obliged."

"Thank you, Nathaniel." Clara ushered him toward the door. "Now we'll give Miss Wigg some privacy." Before she pulled the door shut, she added, "Take your time. We've got almost an hour until dinner is ready."

Yetta removed her hat and placed it atop the dresser. Then she turned and looked around the quiet room. She couldn't believe she had it all to herself. She'd never had her own room before. Within a few minutes, Yetta had things unpacked and everything put away, save for the clean outfit, which she laid out on the bed. She chose her deep-blue dress; it was the nicest one she'd brought. She was hoping to make a better impression at dinner.

As Yetta began to disrobe, she caught a glimpse in the mirror. She wondered if Nathaniel had been as horrified by her appearance. "Oh dear."

A clean set of towels lay folded at the foot of the bed. Standing in her undergarments, Yetta washed up. The feeling of warm water on her skin was refreshing after days of travel. Next, she moved on to her hair, releasing it from the bun and undoing the braid. After brushing it out, she pinned back the front, leaving the rest down.

Yetta slipped into her dress and checked herself in the mirror. She smoothed at the skirt. It didn't look bad for being rolled up and stuffed in a trunk for so long.

Then with a pinch to the cheeks and a dab of tinted pomade to her lips, she was ready.

Chapter Five

Nathaniel tugged at his wool pants. *Gosh, these things are uncomfortable to sit in.*

He'd changed into his Sunday clothes and now waited for Yetta in the parlor. Their initial meeting had been brief. He was anxious to start getting to know Miss Yetta Wigg.

He heard footsteps on the stairs and straightened with anticipation.

A moment later she appeared in the doorway.

She looked like an angel. Her hair lay in silky waves halfway to her waist, looking like threads of gold against her blue dress.

Was this the same woman?

Nathaniel's lips parted. But it was as if he'd forgotten how to speak. He snapped his mouth shut and jumped to his feet. It seemed he'd also forgotten his manners.

"Miss Wigg, don't you look…" He stumbled for the right word. *Ravishing.*

She must have known what he was thinking because her rosy cheeks darkened against her porcelain skin. She smiled. "Please, call me Yetta."

"Very well, Yetta," he said, bowing his head. Breathing easier, he tried again. "You look lovely."

"Thank you, Mr.—"

"Ah ah," he interrupted with a grin. "Nathaniel."

She smiled. "Of course, Nathaniel."

A bell rang outside.

Yetta turned her head to listen.

Nathaniel explained, "That's Clara letting Simpson know it's time for dinner." He extended an arm toward the dining room. "Shall we?"

Yetta turned and Nathaniel placed a hand at the small of her back, escorting her into the other room. Ever since he'd touched her earlier, he'd thought of nothing else. At first, he equated it to the fact that he had not touched a woman in a very long time. But now, judging by the warm sensation making its way through his body, he knew that it had more to do with this particular woman, rather than her gender.

As they entered the dining room, Clara placed a platter in the center of the table. "Hope you like chicken-fixins."

"Why yes," Yetta answered. "I'm so looking forward to a warm meal. I swear, if I never see another sandwich that'll be just fine with me. That's practically all I've eaten since I left New York. Well, besides a few apples."

Nathaniel offered Yetta a chair, pulling it out for her. She gave a nod and sat. Then he moved to the chair adjacent, taking the seat at the head of the table.

Simpson entered the dining room, and Clara directed him to a seat. "You and I will sit over here, if that's okay with you."

"Heck, I'll sit in the latrine for your chicken-fixins," Simpson joked.

"John!" Clara scolded. "Not at the dinner table."

"I ain't sittin' yet," Simpson cackled.

Yetta giggled.

"What's gotten into you?" Clara groaned as he took his seat catty-corner from Yetta. Her expression softened. "I'm sorry, Miss Wigg. It seems my husband has forgotten his manners. I guess it's been a while since we've had a guest for dinner." She sat across from Yetta.

"Please, everyone call me Yetta," she said eloquently. Then to Clara, she added, "And I've worked with young children who love to make jokes on that very subject, so it will take a lot more than that to offend me."

"Hear that, John," Clara said, nudging him with her elbow, "your humor's akin to small children."

Simpson put an arm around his wife and squeezed her. While her face scrunched, his held a huge grin. "Well, you know I'm a kid at heart," he said, planting a kiss on her cheek. A smile spread across Clara's face.

Yetta and Nathaniel laughed.

Nathaniel loved the older couple dearly. And most of all, he wanted a relationship like theirs. With the addition of children though. Sadly, the Simpsons were never able to have children of their own. Maybe that's why Clara was like a mother to Nathaniel and his brothers—they were filling a hole.

Nathaniel served Yetta first, filling her plate with chicken and dressing. Then he filled his plate and passed the serving dish on to Clara. As he placed his napkin across his lap, he opened the conversation.

"So how was your trip? Anything interesting happen along the way?"

"The trip was long but pretty uneventful."

"Nathaniel said you were a teacher in New York," Clara said.

. . .

Yetta's Yearning

Nerves had Yetta smoothing the napkin in her lap and fondling the edges. The fact that she was simply famished added to the moment. She smiled politely and answered, "Yes, I was."

Clara passed the dish to her husband. "Did you like teaching?"

"Yes. I enjoy teaching the younger children most," Yetta answered.

The moment Simpson returned the dish to the center of the table, Clara gave the go-ahead for everyone to dig in.

Nathaniel swallowed a bite and said, "Tell us about the school you taught at."

"Oh, the Wigg School and Foundling Home was wonderful," Yetta answered, remembering fondly. "As I said in my letter, I grew up at the school—most of the teachers did. It was very important to Madam Wigg that every child has the opportunity for a good education. That's something she instilled in all of us." She paused a moment, taking another bite and preparing herself to broach the subject of opening her own school since she'd neglected to mention it in her letters. "I would like to open my own school someday to continue the ideals of the Wigg School."

"That sounds ambitious," Simpson said between chews while hunched over his plate with a fork in one hand and a knife in the other.

"It is," Yetta answered happily. "It's the reason the idea of becoming a mail-order bride even came up. It was a way for us to move on and start our own lives and families, and of course, our own schools."

"How many of you became brides?" Clara asked.

"A couple dozen of us." Yetta dabbed the corners of her mouth with her napkin. "We were of the first group of foundlings at the school—all grown now—and with us moving on, there is room for others to grow and teach. Madam Wigg also offered to bequeath a sizable gift to help maintain a school which continues her teachings—in that all children deserve education."

"Wow, that is very kind of her," Nathaniel said. He reached over and placed his hand atop hers. "I will help in any way I can." The feel of his hand on her skin was nice, but it was the sincerity in his eyes that warmed Yetta's heart.

For a moment she didn't think she could break free from his gaze. What was this hold he had over her? Why was it hard to breathe?

"Enough about me," she said, ending the moment. "I want to know more about you and Triple Peak Ranch. For instance, how did it get that name?"

Nathaniel seemed to have a hard time moving on from the moment as well. He looked down at his plate. "Oh, well, I, um," he stuttered, pushing food around his plate. Yetta lowered her eyes in an attempt to hide her smile. "Because of the view of the mountains from here. There are three very distinct points jutting out above the rest of the range."

Nodding, Yetta took another bite of her dinner.

Clara spoke up. "Nathaniel built everything he has from the ground up. With no help from his family," she added with bite.

"My family is in the cattle business. I knew that was my future," he added as an afterthought. "But I wanted to break out on my own, not rely on their money and success. Wanted to earn my own money to buy my own land and start my own business."

"And you were able to do that with gold mining?" Yetta asked. She'd seen newspaper headlines about gold in the

West, but it seemed unreal to talk to someone who had been a part of such a thing.

"Sure was," he answered. "But I think we were just lucky."

"We?"

"I partnered up with an old friend, Sebastian Carter, to come here from Texas." Nathaniel sat back in his chair. "Sebastian is sticking with it. He enjoys the work." Nathaniel guffawed. "Not me. It's a hard life. And I'd rather work above ground than under it."

"And it's no place to start a family," Clara added.

"Never mind the fact that there are no single women hanging around the mining camps," Nathaniel said. "Even in town, there aren't many single women. Unless you count Toothless Theresa. But at sixty-something, I doubt she could give me the family I desire," he said with a smile.

"Toothless Theresa." Simpson shuddered. "And let me tell you," he said, waving his fork, "she's got a personality to match. Best not get on the wrong side of that woman."

"Duly noted," Yetta said.

"You know, I just had an idea," Nathaniel said, his brow wrinkling in thought. He sat back in his chair. "There's a large camp about twenty minutes from here—out on Nolan Gulch. They've got a bunch of families, and the only education those children get is from their mothers. I bet they would love the idea of bringing in a teacher and setting up a formal school."

Yetta perked up in her seat. "Really?"

"We could take a ride out there tomorrow, if you'd like."

"I would like that very much."

"Well, then it is decided," Nathaniel said, patting the table.

Without another word, Yetta finished her dinner. Her

mind raced with excitement, though she tried not to get carried away with ideas before she saw who and what she'd be working with.

AFTER DINNER, Yetta helped clear the dishes. She was used to helping out at the orphanage, knew her way around a kitchen. Although, she didn't have the patience or talent for cooking like Olivia with her breads or Katriona and Vera with most anything else.

Then it occurred to Yetta, this would be *her* kitchen. Her eyes roamed around the room.

"Do you like to cook?" Clara asked as she made up a plate of food with the leftovers.

"It's okay. Although, I could probably use some help, if you're willing."

"Of course," Clara said. "And I'll be sure to share Nathaniel's favorites with you."

Yetta smiled. "That would be lovely, thank you." She paused a moment, then asked, "Who's that plate for?"

"This is for Jacob. He's a ranch hand," Clara answered. "Has a bed out in the barn. Sometimes he eats with us. I thought I'd make up a plate and run it out to him."

Yetta stepped up to the sink to do the dishes, but Clara stopped her. "I've got these tonight. You've had a long trip. Relax."

"That's okay, I can—"

"No, no," Clara interjected as she wiped her hands on a small towel and tossed it on the counter. "Tonight, you're a guest. How about we move to the parlor for coffee and dessert and I'll clean up later?"

Yetta smiled. "Well, if you insist."

. . .

Yetta's Yearning

THE FOUR OF them continued their conversation in the parlor, enjoying coffee and blueberry pie. Yetta had never felt so grown up. Refined.

Yetta lasted almost an hour before her lids felt heavy and her attention began to wane. The idea of sleeping in a real bed tonight delighted her. She waited for a lull in the conversation.

"If you don't mind, I think I'd like to retire," she said as she stood from her place on the settee.

"Of course," Nathaniel said, rushing to his feet.

Simpson followed, standing gentlemanly for her to leave the room.

"Goodnight, dear," Clara said. "Let me know if you need anything."

Nathaniel walked Yetta to the bottom of the stairs. "I had a wonderful evening."

She gazed up into his slate gray eyes. They stood out against his dark eyebrows. "I did too."

Nathaniel took her hand and raised it between them. He held her gaze as he dipped his head. "May I?"

Yetta's gaze moved from his eyes to his full bottom lip, then to a dimple in the middle of his chin. "Yes," she answered.

Heat rose up the back of her neck as he pressed his lips to her hand. His lips were warm and moist, and she imagined them on her own. Suddenly her body was responding in ways that were entirely new to her. She was feeling sensations that were wonderful and scary at the same time.

"Goodnight, Yetta." His voice was soft and silky.

Yetta had to get out of there before she did things that were unbecoming of an unmarried woman. "Goodnight," she said, turning on her heel and scurrying up the stairs.

Chapter Six

It was a beautiful day for a ride. Nathaniel waited for Yetta out front, with the wagon hitched and a picnic lunch packed and loaded, courtesy of Clara. He looked forward to introducing Yetta to the mining community today, the one he'd been a part of. A community that would always hold a place in his heart. They were good people—hard workers and big dreamers. He also looked forward to showing off his bride-to-be.

The front door opened, and Yetta stepped out, wearing a medium-blue calico dress with lace along the neckline. Nathaniel smiled. She looked lovely. She headed down the steps and was making her way to the wagon when Nathaniel spotted Harley coming out of the barn.

As the shepherd moved closer to Yetta, Nathaniel held his breath. He hadn't mentioned that he had a dog and wondered how she'd react. Although, he remembered she'd said that she loved animals. Just then, Yetta turned and caught sight of the shepherd. Nathaniel took a step forward, ready to intervene if she didn't take kindly to his pet.

Yetta's Yearning

Imagine his surprise when Yetta dropped to her knees and squealed in delight as Harley raced into her outstretched arms. He knew then and there that this woman was a keeper.

"Who's this?" she asked as he approached.

He bent and patted the dog on the head. It made his heart happy to see his two ladies getting along. "This is Harley."

"I love her!" Yetta pressed her lips together and squeezed her eyes shut as the pooch went in for kisses, nearly toppling her over. But she still smiled.

Nathaniel laughed and offered her a hand up. "Sorry about that."

"It is quite all right," she said, brushing herself off.

Nathaniel pulled out a hanky and stepped closer. "Here," he said, lifting her chin with his other hand. "Let me get that."

Yetta gazed up at him as he wiped her face gently where Harley had licked her. He found himself gazing back, his hand still going through the motions. He was lost in her eyes. He'd been confused on their color. They seemed to change with the lighting and her surroundings. The first time he'd laid eyes on her, her could've sworn they were green with a touch of gold. But now, they were as blue as her dress.

Yetta released a breath, her lips parting slightly.

He desperately wanted to kiss her.

Sucking in a ragged breath, Nathaniel stepped back and gestured toward the wagon, bringing their moment to a crashing halt. "Shall we?"

THE WAGON MOVED slow but at a steady pace. The road twisted and turned up the five-mile incline toward Nolan

Gulch. The scenery was breathtaking, and he'd seen it a million times. He wondered what a girl from the East thought.

Nathaniel glanced her way. She was sitting up tall, practically on the edge of the bench, and had a big smile on her face. Maybe this was the kind of adventure she was looking for. He was happy to oblige.

As they approached the edge of camp, the wagon slowed.

"We'll park her here and walk in," he said, engaging the brake.

Nathaniel hopped down from the wagon and offered a hand to Yetta. After what had happened yesterday, he wasn't sure if she'd take the help. So, he was surprised when she bent and placed her hands on his shoulders for support. He grabbed her waist and lowered her gently, making sure not to let his hands linger this time. It wasn't easy.

They walked down the wide center aisle between rows of once-white tents and small cabins, dodging mud and ruts. While he thought she was a little overdressed for such a place, she didn't seem to notice. Nathaniel liked that about her. She didn't act like she was above others who may have been less fortunate. And that was something he might've expected from a well-educated woman from a big city in the East.

Nathaniel pointed out familiar faces and shared a quick tale or two as they made their way farther into the camp.

"That's Adelaide Bouchard," he said of a woman doing laundry in a wooden bucket. She looked up and smiled as they passed. "She has two children. Makes the best rabbit stew."

Yetta jumped out of the way as two young boys ran by pushing a large hoop with a stick.

"That's Jonah and Isaiah. They belong to Mary Thatcher," he said, pointing to a woman down the way who was busy hanging wet clothing from a line.

They came to a woman standing in front of a cabin, balancing a pig-tailed toddler on her hip. "Nathaniel," she greeted with a smile, "it's good to see you."

"You too, Mrs. Jennings," Nathaniel replied.

"If you're looking for Sebastian, I think you're out of luck," she said. "He's gone a little farther north, prospecting new sites."

"Oh, I'm sorry I missed him," Nathaniel said, "but actually, you're the one I wanted to talk to today. Do you have a few minutes?"

Before she could answer, three children burst from the door. "Don't go far—lunch is almost ready," Mrs. Jennings warned her two as they ran off. Then to the third, she said, "Michael, your mother is looking for you." She repositioned the toddler on her hip and looked back to Nathaniel. "Sure, I've got a few minutes. Come in; let's sit down."

Nathaniel and Yetta followed Mrs. Jennings inside. Three single cots and a double lined the wall to the left. A woodstove sat in the center toward the back, and a small handmade table with benches were located to the right. The woman put the toddler on the floor and handed her a worn cloth doll. The adults sat at the table.

When Nathaniel had the woman's attention, he began his introduction. "I'd like you to meet my bride, Yetta Wigg. She's a teacher from New York City."

The woman smiled. "Wow, a real teacher," she said. "It's nice to meet you, Miss Wigg."

"And this is Margery Jennings," Nathaniel added.

"Nice to meet you as well," Yetta replied. Her eyes moved adoringly to the child. "And who's this little one?"

"That's Emily, my youngest," Mrs. Jennings said. "My middle two almost ran you over outside, and my oldest is off somewhere."

Yetta smiled. "How old are they?"

"Two, five, seven, and ten."

Nathaniel glanced at Yetta and back to Mrs. Jennings. "Yetta would really love to continue teaching, so we came here to run an idea by you." The woman cocked her head in interest. "What would you think about opening a school near the camp?"

"I would love for my children to go to a real school. Be taught by a real teacher, but…" Mrs. Jennings flashed a skeptical smile. "But I don't think that's something we could afford to finance, Nathaniel." She turned her look to Yetta. "I'm sorry. I'm sure you're a fine teacher, but the families here don't—"

Nathaniel raised a hand, cutting her off. "No, wait, I think you've misunderstood. The cost to the families would be…" He looked to Yetta.

"Minimal," Yetta answered. "I believe every child should be given the opportunity to learn, and that means that I would never turn a child away for their parents' inability to pay."

"Why—" The woman's brow knitted. "I mean, how. How can you afford to be so generous? And you don't even know us."

Nathaniel sat back, letting Yetta take the floor. He beamed with pride.

"It is the ideal I was brought up with, and I don't have to know you. If Nathaniel says you are good people, then I trust him." Yetta turned her gaze to Nathaniel and smiled. "As far as the finances, I can get help with that in due time. But meanwhile, I don't see why we couldn't start simple. All I'd require is children with an attitude for learning and some sort of shelter," she said, turning her palm and her eyes toward the ceiling.

"I was thinking the tent y'all use for church service and other events," Nathaniel added.

Mrs. Jennings smiled, big and broad. "That might just work."

"How many children would you say you have in this camp between the ages of, let's say, five and ten?" Yetta asked.

"Hmm." The woman sat thoughtfully, counting on her fingers. "Around nine or ten."

"How about eleven and up, who might still be school-aged?"

"Some of the older children are already working, but I'd say maybe seven."

"Perfect," Yetta replied with a smile. Nathaniel couldn't take his eyes off her. He loved the way her lips moved when she spoke. And the way her smile reached her eyes. "That sounds very doable."

Nathaniel stepped back into the conversation. "How do you suggest we approach the other families about this, Mrs. Jennings?"

The child began to fuss. Mrs. Jennings scooped her off the floor and placed her on her knee. "Why don't you let me handle that?"

"All right," Nathaniel said.

Bouncing the fussy child on her knee, the mother asked, "Could we meet again one week from today?"

"Sure." He looked to Yetta, who nodded in agreement.

Mrs. Jennings stood, propping the child on her hip again. "I'll talk with the other mothers and see what kind of response I get. If you could come back next week around the same time to present a plan, I'll have an audience for you," she said, wrapping up the conversation.

"That would be great. Thank you so much," Nathaniel said as he rose to his feet. Yetta followed, and they started for the door. "And please tell Sebastian of our visit. Maybe we could meet up with him next time."

Yetta left the Jennings cabin feeling optimistic. She was excited to get home and start jotting down some plans. With the numbers she was looking at and their limited accommodations and supplies, Yetta's first thought was to break the children into two age groups. She could teach the younger children in the morning and the older ones in the afternoon.

Suddenly, Nathaniel grabbed her by the arm and pulled her to the side. Yetta had been so engrossed in thought that she'd nearly stepped into a mud puddle.

"Sorry, I guess you didn't hear my warning," he said. "And I didn't want you to ruin your fancy shoes."

Fancy? Yetta didn't consider anything she owned to be fancy. At least not by New York standards. She began to look around at the other women in the camp. Study them. They wore simple dresses. No lace trim or decorative buttons. And their shoes didn't have buttons either, or a heel. They were brown like the mud, and they tied. She suddenly felt a bit overdressed.

Yetta felt her cheeks flush. "Thanks. That would have been embarrassing."

They reached the wagon parked at the edge of camp, and Yetta looked back. "So, you used to live here?"

"Sure did." Nathaniel sighed and glanced around. "Seems like a lifetime ago."

"And all these families are here for the gold?"

"Yep."

Her eyes narrowed. She didn't understand this business. "How does that work? I mean, do they *work* together?"

"Some do," he answered, stopping to help her into the wagon. Once he was seated beside her, he continued, "But most have personal claims. They are here for hard rock mining—looking for a main vein. And then there are a few here for placer gold."

"What's placer gold?"

"That's when the gold has broken away from the original vein and been moved by stream flow. Then the flecks and nuggets get deposited along the stream bed amongst the sand and gravel." Yetta could tell he liked sharing his knowledge. "Have you heard of panning?"

"Oh, yes. I think so."

"That's the technique they use to mine for placer gold. Another would be to use what's called a sluice box. Both a little less hard labor than hard rock mining. And take a lot less initial cost and equipment. Of course, the payout is usually less."

Nathaniel went on for a while, telling her all about his own adventures in mining. She loved the sound of his voice. Smooth, deep, and silky. She could listen to him for hours.

He steered the wagon off the main path. The new path followed the top of a ridge. A quiet stream lay at the bottom of the slope. He directed the horses toward a patch of trees, and they stopped in the shade, like they'd been here before.

Nathaniel rested his elbows on his knees and released a long breath as he looked out over the valley. "Pretty, isn't it?"

"It's beautiful," Yetta answered. She loved the way the wild flowers and grasses swayed in the light wind. She lifted her chin and closed her eyes, enjoying the breeze and the cooler temperature out of the sun.

"I love it here," he said. "It's where I come to think." After another moment of quiet, Nathaniel engaged the brake and reached behind the bench seat for the basket. "Would you care to join me for a picnic?" He simpered.

Yetta was excited for the picnic. Her first with a gentleman. But after the moment they'd shared back at the ranch this morning, she was starting to wonder if they should've brought a chaperone. Sure, he was her betrothed, but they weren't married yet.

Chapter Seven

Nathaniel had been coming to this spot overlooking the creek for years, but today was the first time he'd ever brought company. His palms began to sweat. What was he thinking, bringing her out here all alone when he had barely been able to contain himself back at the ranch?

They moved to a shade tree closer to the water, the sun behind them. Nathaniel laid out a blanket and placed the basket in the center. He waited for Yetta to sit first. She sat toward the edge, her knees bent and curled to one side. He could tell she was nervous, so he knew he had to watch himself.

Leaving plenty of space between them—for his own good as well as hers—he sat down. He stretched his legs out in front of him, ankles crossed, and leaned back, bracing himself with his arms behind him.

Clara had wrapped the food in tea towels: a fresh loaf of bread in one and a couple of her homemade pickles and left-over chicken in the other. Yetta began unwrapping and laying out the food. She tore the small loaf into two pieces and offered one to Nathaniel.

"Thank you," he said, sitting forward and taking a bite. With legs bent, he rested his forearms on his knees and stared off, enjoying the view while he reflected on their morning. "I think our conversation with Mrs. Jennings couldn't have gone any better." He bit into the bread again. "She's well respected, so I'm confident she'll see it through and get the other families on board."

"That would be wonderful," Yetta said. "Thank you for taking time out of your day to bring me out here. I hope it wasn't too much trouble."

"No trouble at all. I wanted to spend the day with you."

Yetta smiled.

"So, what do you think of Colorado so far?"

Yetta gazed off. "It's beautiful." She brought her eyes back to Nathaniel. "And so quiet. I thought I was going to have a hard time going to sleep without the city street noise. But I passed out as soon as my head hit the pillow." She laughed.

Nathaniel loved the way she tossed her head back when she laughed, and the sound was angelic. He found her free spirit refreshing.

They enjoyed conversation over lunch. So much, in fact, that they'd done more talking than they had eating. But hearing her speak of life in the big city and living with so many sisters was fascinating.

At the moment, Yetta was telling him about a fellow teacher named Abigail, who had two children and had gone to Montana as a mail-order bride. Yetta shared how delighted she was to hear that everything had worked out well for Abigail and her children. She'd finally gotten the happy family she deserved.

Nathaniel didn't mean to let his mind wander, but it

did. He found himself overwhelmed with want. He wanted a family. And he wanted it with Yetta.

He never would've guessed he could find the perfect woman by placing an ad for a mail-order bride. To think of all the possible ways this could've gone… How had he been so lucky? On the surface it was easy to see that Yetta was beautiful, vibrant, and refined. But today he'd seen so much more. He pictured the loving way she'd looked at little Emily. In that moment he knew she would make a wonderful mother to his children.

Nathaniel finished chewing the last of his chicken, wiped his hands on his pants, and got to one knee. "Miss Yetta Wigg, will you marry me?" Yetta put down the slice of chicken she'd been holding and looked up at him in wonderment. "I mean right away. Today even," he explained with excitement. "I know I said we could wait, but I don't want to, I want you to be my wife."

YETTA'S BREATH caught in her throat. While she'd already agreed to become his wife, hearing the words—seeing the emotion behind them—sent her heart aflutter. This was a moment she wanted to remember forever. The perfect setting. The perfect man. It seemed like a scene from one of the many novels she'd read.

She'd been so caught up in the moment that she suddenly realized she hadn't answered.

"Yes." She didn't know whether she wanted to laugh or cry. "Yes, I will marry you."

"You've made me a very happy man."

Seeing the huge smile on his face brought tears to her eyes.

His smile turned to concern, and he reached for her arm. "What is it? What's wrong?"

"Nothing is wrong." She smiled through the tears. "I'm just…so happy."

Nathaniel's hand slid down her arm. He took her hand and pulled her to her knees. Then his hands moved up and cradled her face. They were warm and large but also tender as he wiped away her tears with his thumbs.

Yetta imagined his hands touching her body in ways—and places—she'd never been touched before. Those places felt warm and tingly. She pulled her bottom lip between her teeth and stifled a moan. His slate gray eyes stared into her almost as if he was in pain. They were hypnotizing.

Yetta let her eyes fall shut, hoping to release herself from their power. But it was no use. She was already under his spell. She pressed her cheek into his hand and nuzzled slightly, running her lips over his palm.

Nathaniel's other hand slid behind her head, his fingers tangling in her hair. She opened her eyes and met his again. His breath came out in a rush as he drew her closer and pressed his lips to hers.

While Yetta was completely inexperienced, her body seemed to know what to do. And with his hands still on her, guiding her, she knew she was safe.

And she knew that she wanted it to happen. Here. Now.

The sun now overhead touched the edge of the blanket as Nathaniel lounged, arms folded behind his head. He couldn't stop smiling.

Yetta glanced over her shoulder at him as she buttoned her dress. Her cheeks were rosy pink, her hair disheveled.

"Stop looking at me like that," she said bashfully.

"I can't help it. You're the most beautiful thing I've

ever laid eyes on."

She giggled.

He raised up onto one elbow. "Are you sure we have to go now?"

"Yes," she answered, shoving his shoulder playfully. "We have to go to town and make this official now that we…" She tucked her chin to her shoulder and peeked through her lashes, her cheeks turning ever redder.

"I'll make an honest woman of ya, I promise," he said with a smile, pulling her back down to him and kissing her again.

"Now, now, Mr. Price," Yetta argued, pushing herself upright, "there will be plenty of time for that after we see the reverend."

"Alright, alright," he said, getting to his feet. "Let's find us a reverend."

Yetta tossed the remains of their picnic into the basket and wandered closer to the water, while Nathaniel scooped up the blanket and folded it. He decided to let her have a quiet moment alone, so he grabbed the basket and headed for the wagon.

He set everything in the back before moving to the front to check on the horses.

"Hey girls," he said, stroking the sides of their heads.

In his peripheral, he saw Yetta approaching. He turned with a smile. "Ready to get hitched?"

His smile dropped and mouth fell open as a cold rush ran through him. He felt as though his heart stopped beating. "Where did you get those?" he asked of the bouquet of small white flowers in her hand.

She looked confused. "Over there." She pointed down the hill. "Why? What's wrong?"

"They call them Death Lilies," he answered, his voice shaky.

Chapter Eight

Yetta released her grip and the flowers fell to the ground. She stared at the palm of her hand through tear-filled eyes as though her own limb was foreign to her.

Nathaniel was all in a panic, looking this way and that.

"You're scaring me," she said.

He pressed at his temples, mumbling to himself, then straightened as an idea hit him. "Go to the water and start rinsing anywhere the flowers came in contact." Stunned, she didn't move. "Go!"

His yell startled her, and she took off down the hill.

Yetta plunged her hand into the water. She swished it back and forth and rubbed it on the rocks, all the while fighting the urge to retch.

A moment later, Nathaniel appeared at her side. "Dry your hand on the grass."

She did as she was told. When it was dry, she looked at him for further instruction. That's when he did the strangest thing.

In Nathaniel's hand was one of the pickles they hadn't eaten. He broke it in half and began rubbing it all over her skin. "I think the vinegar will help absorb the poisons."

Yetta watched his face as he took great care in tending to her. There was no mistaking his love. She was angry with herself for causing him worry. "I'm sorry, I didn't know," she whispered.

He stopped what he was doing and looked her in the eye. His expression softened. "Oh, sweetheart, it's not your fault."

She felt her lip quiver.

He hugged her tight, then calmed as he went back to crushing and rubbing pickle juice on her hand and in between her fingers. "I'm sorry." He shook his head. "I was just so scared. They say that even touching the Death Lily can cause serious illness. I'm sure you're going to be fine."

"Do you still want to marry me?"

"What?" His eyes snapped to hers. "Of course! Why would you ask that?"

"You're not disappointed in me?"

"No!" He put his free hand up to the side of her face and gazed lovingly into her eyes. "I knew the moment you came into my life that we were meant to be together," he said, finishing with a gentle kiss.

Yetta's chest hurt with love for this man. And suddenly she couldn't imagine her life without him. She didn't even care if she lost her hand as long as they were together.

Nathaniel turned her hand over, inspecting it. "I think we're good here." He wiped his hands on his pants and smiled. "Still want to go to town today?"

Tears filled her eyes once more as she nodded. She wouldn't keep this man waiting.

A SHORT TIME later they pulled into town. Yetta hadn't

seen much of it the first time she was here. It wasn't what she had expected—a sleepy frontier town. Nor was it the more extreme saloons and gun-slinging spectacle that she'd heard was common in the West.

It looked like a charming little town, bustling with activity. But not at all like New York City, with its paved and cobblestone streets and people dressed to the nines. Here, instead of men in grays, blues, and blacks, they wore various shades of brown. Even the women wore subdued colors and simple bonnets for practicality instead of fashion.

"So, this is Colorado Springs," Nathaniel announced. "It's a nice little town—still growing. We get some miners coming through on their way to Colorado City, which is the main supply hub. But the Springs is beginning to attract the tourists."

They continued making their way down what seemed to be a main street, with narrow alleys splitting off every now and again. A simple white church came into view up ahead.

"If we're lucky, Reverend Hale hasn't left for supper yet. He usually goes next door to the Chandler Boarding House."

The wagon stopped out front. Nathaniel hopped out and helped Yetta down. They hurried up the stairs and into the church. The door closed with a knock, and an older man, who Yetta assumed was the reverend, stepped from a doorway in the corner.

"Well, hello, Nathaniel," the man said. "What brings you by?"

"Reverend," Nathaniel greeted with a nod. He grabbed Yetta by the hand. "We'd like to get married."

"Right now?"

"Do you have a few minutes?" Nathaniel asked.

He glanced at the clock on the wall. "Sure, I've got some time."

While the reverend prepared for the marriage ceremony, Nathaniel went next door to fetch a witness.

Alone in the quiet church, Yetta inhaled a deep breath and sat in a pew. She couldn't believe it was happening—she really and truly was getting married. Catching a whiff, she sighed to herself. *This would be so much more romantic if I didn't smell like pickles.*

Nerves had her fidgeting. She removed the pins from her hair and ran her fingers through it, pulling it into a chignon and fastening the pins again. She realized her knees were bouncing furiously, so she placed her hands on her lap and steadied them. With another deep breath, she smoothed her dress with her palms. Her right one itched a little. But if that was the worst of the effects from the poisonous flowers, then she couldn't complain.

The floorboards creaked, announcing she was no longer alone.

Yetta turned in her seat.

Nathaniel had returned. He stood in the aisle with a smile on his face and a bouquet of pale-pink roses in his hands. Yetta beamed. It was as if he'd read her mind. He held them out for her taking.

Yetta took the bouquet with both hands and buried her face in them, inhaling their intense, sweet fragrance. Gone was the assault of vinegar on her nose.

"Are we ready?" Reverend Hale asked from the altar.

Nathaniel passed a glance over his shoulder. An older, dark-haired woman had followed him into the church. She was broad through the chest and had the waist to support it. She removed her white apron and set it on the back pew, then looked down and gave her dark-grey work dress the once-over.

"Mrs. Chandler has agreed to be our witness," Nathaniel said, extending an arm, welcoming her forward.

"Although I have one condition," she said, her voice bold and gravelly. Authoritative.

Yetta tensed, worried the woman didn't approve of her. Nathaniel's brow furrowed. "Condition?"

"Yes," Mrs. Chandler answered, letting a smile creep out. "You must join us for supper. We'll make it a *wedding* supper."

Yetta released her breath and smiled, as did Nathaniel. He looked at Yetta as he answered the older woman, "Of course. How kind of you."

The ceremony itself was quick and simple. And even though she was in an everyday dress and hadn't had a proper bath in a week, Yetta felt like a princess standing beside Nathaniel. Especially the first time he introduced her as his wife when they arrived at the boarding house.

Mrs. Chandler set two extra places at the table and told everyone where to sit as they entered the dining room. There were seven people, not including Yetta and Nathaniel. Mr. and Mrs. Chandler, and Reverend Hale, of course. The others were guests staying at the boarding house. Edgar Salzman, a middle-aged gentleman and his younger travel partner, who was introduced more formally as Mr. Blackwell. They were in town for a few weeks while Mr. Salzman worked on plans to build a hotel. The other two were Louis Jones and his seventeen-year-old daughter Ava, who'd traveled from Illinois in search of a new life.

Yetta was seated next to Ava, and while she shared her relief in finding someone close in age to talk to, Ava nearly wept.

"You have no idea," she said with the slightest hint of a French accent. She leaned toward Yetta, keeping her voice low. "I've been in town two weeks and barely been outside this boarding house."

Yetta's hand went to her heart. Just the thought made her claustrophobic. "You can't be serious."

Ava nodded. Her eyes scanned the people around the table. She lowered her voice even more. "Don't get me wrong, they're all nice people. Well…" she hesitated, her eyes stopping on Mr. Blackwell on the opposite corner. "I'm not sure about that one. I don't know why, but he gives me a bad feeling."

Yetta watched him for a moment. Curious.

Silver tinging against glass called everyone's attention to the reverend. He gave the blessing and welcomed everyone to dig in. The food was delicious and the conversation delightful. Yetta could tell that she and Ava would be fast friends. This unexpected celebration to their unexpected day was nothing short of perfect.

It was almost dark by the time they returned from the long day. Harley greeted them as the wagon pulled up, just like always. Nathaniel helped Yetta down and went to call on Jacob to unhitch and put away the team.

When he returned, he found Yetta sitting on the steps, her arm resting on the shepherd beside her. He grinned at the sight.

As he reached the bottom of the steps, Harley rushed down to him.

"That's my girl." He patted her on the head, then pointed toward the barn. "Go help Jacob," he commanded in a lively manner. The dog ran off, and Nathaniel turned and climbed the steps.

Yetta stood and joined him on the porch.

Nathaniel pressed the latch on the door handle with his

thumb and the door swung open. The house was quiet and dark. Tonight, they had it all to themselves.

He turned to Yetta and scooped her up in his arms. She let out a squeal of delight and wrapped her arms around his neck as he carried her over the threshold. Once inside, he kicked the door shut and continued up the stairs, finally setting her on the bed they would share.

NATHANIEL WOKE JUST BEFORE SUNRISE. Seeing Yetta's head on the pillow next to him brought a smile to his face. Content, he watched her sleep for a few minutes, although he was relieved when she stirred a bit. "Good morning, wife."

Her eyes fluttered open. "Good morning, husband."

"Did you sleep well?"

"I did. You?"

"Best sleep of my life," he answered.

"Would you like some breakfast?"

"I would. I'm famished." He flashed a crooked smile and tucked his hands behind his head. "Hey… I don't even know if you can cook."

"Well, I can," she said, sitting up and swinging her feet over the edge of the bed. "Nothing fancy, unless you count cooking for a small army fancy," she joked as she reached for her dress, which she'd tossed haphazardly on the chair a few feet away.

Nathaniel got out of bed and pulled on his pants.

"What are you doing?" She slipped her dress over her head. "You should stay and rest."

"I can help," he said as he fastened the buttons.

"It's okay. I can handle this." She pulled her hair into a bun.

He could see that his new wife was the determined

type. He stepped toward her and rested his hands on her hips. "I'd rather be by your side helping in the kitchen than up here all alone."

Finally conceding, they made their way down to the kitchen.

"Clara made sure the kitchen was pretty well stocked before you arrived, but let me know if there's anything else you need," he said as she began looking in cupboards and checking out the lay of the land. "Feel free to rearrange the kitchen to your liking," he added.

Nathaniel helped gather the ingredients and cookware for a simple breakfast of eggs, toast, and bacon, but he left the cooking to Yetta. And since his coffee usually had the consistency of sludge, he happily let her make that as well.

He pulled out a chair and sat sideways to the table, using it to rest one arm. He watched her move around the kitchen. She looked both confident and uncertain at the same time. And while he admired her grace and beauty made prominent by her fancy city clothes, he knew she was going to need more appropriate attire for working the homestead. That way she could save her dresses for special occasions.

Gold locks came loose from her bun and fell into her face as she turned the bacon in the pan. With spatula in hand, she tried to use her forearm to brush her hair back.

Nathaniel stepped up behind her. He wrapped one arm around her waist and lifted his other hand to tuck her hair behind her ear. "Mind if I help?" he said softly.

Yetta's head listed to the side, freeing her neck as his fingers lingered, tracing a line from her ear to her shoulder. He touched his lips to her skin, and suddenly he had a thirst that needed quenching.

. . .

Yetta found it strange that less than twenty-four hours earlier she'd never been intimate with a man, but now all it took was a simple touch to send her body into a frenzy. She was able to control herself until he pressed his body against hers.

She turned in his arms, and his mouth found hers. He kissed her with wild abandon, his tongue plunging in and out, as she struggled between keeping up or giving in and letting him devour her.

Her back arched as she let out a small moan. Nathaniel swung her around, lifting her and planting her buttocks on the table.

A few minutes later, the smell of something burning caught their attention.

"Uh-oh, not the bacon," Nathaniel joked.

Holding his pants up with one hand, he grabbed a towel and moved the pan off the heat. Yetta pulled the toast from the oven, then grabbed the spatula and flipped the eggs.

After the rush, they stopped and looked at each other, a mixture of embarrassment and fluster on their faces.

"Breakfast is ready," Yetta sang.

To which they both busted out laughing.

After they finished eating, Yetta got up from her chair and began clearing the plates.

Nathaniel stood, announcing, "I've gotta get to work." He leaned in and planted a kiss on her cheek before heading for the door.

"Wait," she said, hearing the panic in her own voice. "When will you be back?"

"We break for lunch around noon." He pulled on his boots and put his hand on the door handle.

She glanced around the room, then gave him an

uneasy look. "What am I supposed to do while you're gone?"

"Oh. Well…" Nathaniel hesitated. He'd obviously picked up on her worry, because he released the handle and turned to her. "Take some time to get settled," he offered. "And you can always go over to the cabin and visit with Clara. I'm sure she'd love to have the company."

"Okay."

"Okay," he repeated. He moved closer and put a hand on her arm. "Are you gonna be all right?"

Yetta nodded and waved her hand. "Yes, of course. I'll be fine." The moment the door closed behind him, she felt an ache in her chest. She missed him already.

She gave herself a moment, then got right to work. A busy mind was a happy mind—at least that's what Wiggie used to say.

She washed the dishes and cleaned up the kitchen, taking note of its layout as she put things away. She didn't feel the need to change a thing. Although, there were a few items she'd like to get for the pantry.

After finding a pad of paper at the desk in the parlor, she returned to the kitchen table and started making a list. She added fabric and sewing supplies. While she wasn't exactly the dressmaker Fae was, she knew she was going to need more dresses. Which reminded her that she desperately needed to do her laundry and take a bath.

She strummed her fingers on the table. "But what to do first?"

Yetta put on her shoes and headed out the door.

Chapter Nine

Simpson and Jacob were already busy maintaining the livestock housed in the barn when Nathaniel joined them after breakfast. The ranch had over a dozen horses and a milking cow, in addition to the cattle herd, most of which were currently grazing in the lower section of the property. With a creek bed on one side and a steep incline on the other, it was enough to keep them somewhat corralled until they were able to get all thousand head sorted and branded. It was a task they'd been preparing for since the cattle arrived less than a week ago.

"Hey," Simpson greeted him. "Didn't see you at all yesterday. Everything all right?"

"More than all right," Nathaniel answered. "Yetta and I went to see Reverend Hale yesterday afternoon."

Simpson's face brightened. "You got hitched? Well, I'll be." He slapped his friend on the back. "Congratulations! Hey, Jake," he called over his shoulder. "Did ya hear that? Nathaniel's a married man."

Jacob stepped out from a stall. "Congratulations, Mr. Price."

"We've gotta celebrate," Simpson said. "You're gonna throw a party, ain't ya?"

Nathaniel beamed. "I hadn't really thought about it, but we should throw a party."

As he saddled up the horses, Nathaniel thought more about the idea of having a celebration. Since everything in his life was coming together, it would be a great opportunity to make a statement in the community. A community that he hoped one day would see him as a key player.

A short time later the three men rode out to the sorting station they'd prepared. Post and rail fencing funneled the herd as Simpson drove them forward on horseback. Coming down the line, Nathaniel marked them with Triple Peak's symbol and Jacob manned the gate. For now, they were separating into two groups: big and small. Nathaniel planned to take some of the larger cattle to auction later in the week.

By noon, Nathaniel was spent. He looked forward to breaking for lunch and seeing how Yetta was making out.

It had been a busy morning for Yetta. She'd gone to Clara after breakfast to ask for guidance. At the Wigg School, there was structure to their days. She knew what had to be done and when. And she realized that was what she needed now.

Structure.

A plan.

And she knew Clara was just the one to help.

Of course, Clara was happy to take Yetta under her wing. And since it was still early in the day, they started right away with morning chores. Yetta quickly realized how little she knew about homestead living. They didn't get their eggs from a vendor or their milk delivered in bottles. Nope. They went to the barn for those things.

They tended to the chickens first; that consisted of feeding, watering, and gathering eggs. But the most important thing she learned was the trick to retrieving the eggs without getting pecked. While it may have started a bit chaotic, she eventually got the hang of it and even got to pet a few of them. And she was proud of herself for not breaking a single egg.

Milking a cow was another new experience for Yetta. And that did not come as easy. Yetta couldn't be sure, but she suspected the person who coined the phrase 'don't cry over spilt milk' had never actually milked a cow. Because it was dang hard, and when you'd been at it for what seemed like an hour, only to the have the cow kick the bucket over...*all* you wanted to do was cry.

The chores got a little easier after that. They changed the bedding, did the wash, and beat the rugs...all before noon.

All morning Yetta had been dying to tell Clara her news, but she thought Nathaniel should tell her. Essentially, she was his family. And as they prepared lunch for the men, Yetta grew surprisingly giddy to see Nathaniel and finally share her secret.

The door opened.

Simpson walked in ahead of the others, his mouth already flapping as he hung his hat by the door, "Did ya hear the news, Clara? They done got hitched!"

Clara's face brightened as she flashed a glance to Yetta. "What? Why didn't you tell me?"

Yetta felt her cheeks flush. Nathaniel hung his hat and came to her rescue, wrapping an arm around her shoulder.

Then Clara turned her gaze on him. "I thought you were going to wait a week."

"What I had said was that I was willing to wait a week or two if it would make her feel more comfortable." He smiled down at Yetta and added, "Turns out neither of us wanted to wait. By the way, Yetta, this is Jacob."

"Howdy, ma'am," Jacob said with hat in hand. He was a nice-looking boy, supposedly a year her junior, but Yetta suspected he had lied about his age to get this job. He looked closer to fifteen.

"Hello, Jacob," Yetta returned.

"I want to hear about the wedding," Clara said, waving her hands.

"All right." Yetta laughed.

The five of them sat at the small table in the kitchen, and Yetta started the story from when they left the camp and stopped for the picnic. While she didn't share *all* the details, she did include the scare with the Death Lilies, to which Clara grabbed Yetta's hands and inspected her palms. The right one had some redness and bumps.

"I have a salve that will fix that right up," Clara said. "Remind me to grab it after we eat."

Nathaniel continued the story from there: the visit to town to see Reverend Hale and the invitation to the boarding house for a wedding supper celebration.

Simpson got in on the conversation. "I said we should throw a party."

Yetta's eyes grew wide. "A party?"

"What do you think of the idea? We could throw a dance in the barn," Nathaniel said. "It would be a great way for you to meet everyone."

Yetta did love a party. But the idea of hosting something of that nature was more than she could handle at the moment.

Nathaniel picked up on her clues. "But we don't have to decide right now," he added.

With great relief, Yetta released the breath she'd been holding, and the conversation moved on to other things. And before she knew it, lunch was over, and the men were returning to work. Which meant so were the women.

After cleaning up the lunch dishes, they got started on their afternoon chores. They worked in the garden, weeding and picking vegetables they'd use for dinner. Clara mentioned there'd be berries ready for canning soon. But that was a task for another day because they needed to get the bread in the oven before retrieving the laundry from the line and taking care of the mending.

Yetta tried not to let on that she was slightly overwhelmed. How was one woman supposed to do all of this? At school, the chores were split up amongst them. And there was always someone around to help.

But Yetta muscled through and did it with a smile, all the while wondering how'd she'd even have time for teaching.

Chapter Ten

The next few days passed in a blur as Nathaniel and Yetta settled into their new way of life. They all had adjusting to do, even Simpson and Clara. It wasn't that long ago that the two of them had lived under the same roof as Nathaniel. Although the biggest change was for Yetta, coming from a home in a big city, surrounded by sisters and children. She knew it would take some time to get used to the quiet.

Yetta was grateful that by the third day she was already getting the hang of things. And by splitting some of the chores with Clara, they both ended up with more time on their hands. That delighted Clara; she hadn't had help before.

Today Yetta was getting a break. Nathaniel was taking her to town to get the things on her list. She was also looking forward to stopping by the boarding house to visit Ava while Nathaniel took care of some business.

Yetta sat on the bench seat of the wagon and watched while Nathaniel climbed in. He sat beside her and picked up the reins. Then he handed them to her.

She held the reins tenderly, as if they would bite, and looked over at him with wide eyes. "I don't know how to drive a wagon."

"I'm going to teach you."

Yetta shook her head. "Oh, I don't know about that…"

"You'll be fine. It's easy," he reassured. "Then you'll be able to drive yourself to town whenever you want…and of course to the camp when you start teaching."

She liked how confident he was that she'd be teaching soon. She took a calming breath and relaxed her shoulders. "Okay."

Before long, Yetta had the hang of it. It helped that the horses seemed to know the routes, and it took only the slightest of touch to lead them in the right direction.

With Nathaniel's guidance, Yetta steered the horses to the front of the mercantile and pulled the reins back gently, until they were taut. The horses slowed to a stop, and Nathaniel engaged the hand brake on his side.

"Very good," he praised Yetta. "You drove us to town. Easy, wasn't it?"

Yetta smiled proudly. "It actually was."

A bell jingled, announcing their presence as they opened the door to the mercantile. A moment later a red-haired woman slipped through a curtain from the back and went behind the counter.

"Hello. What can I do ya for?" The woman spoke with a bit of an Irish accent.

Nathaniel stepped forward as Yetta dug the folded list from her reticule. "We have a list of some dry goods we need, and my wife would like to look at your fabrics."

Yetta loved hearing Nathaniel say those words "my wife." It made her heart beat faster.

"Didn't realize ya were married," the woman said.

"Only, just." Nathaniel put his hand on the small of Yetta's back. "This is my wife, Yetta."

"Nice t'meet ya, Yetta. I'm Shannon O'Brien," she said with a smile, then she called over her shoulder. "George, could ya come up front?"

"Yep!" a deep voice answered, followed by the sound of a chair scraping across the floor. He appeared from behind the curtain. "What's up?"

Mrs. O'Brien regarded the couple standing in front of her. "I wanted ya to meet Yetta, Mr. Price's new wife." She glanced back at the man. "Yetta, this is me husband, George."

"Nice to meet you both."

Mrs. O'Brien passed Mr. O'Brien the list. "Could ya start on this while I help Yetta?" She didn't wait for an answer. She stepped from behind the counter, gesturing toward the far corner. "Right this way."

Yetta followed.

"These are the fabrics we have on hand," Mrs. O'Brien said. "We can always order more if there's something specific you're looking for."

"I'm sure what you have will be fine," Yetta said with a smile. "I just need a work dress and apron." Yetta had talked to Clara about her plans to make more dresses, but she decided to follow Clara's advice and start with one.

"Very well, then. Our notions are back here," Mrs. O'Brien said as she spun around, directing Yetta's attention to the small bins lining the shelves on the wall behind them. "Let me know if ya need any help." And with that, she rejoined the men at the front.

As Yetta looked through the bolts of fabric, she heard the bell ring. Two women walked in. They chatted as they browsed, clearly not on a specific mission. They seemed to be friends enjoying a day together. Suddenly Yetta missed her sisters. While she was beyond happy with Nathaniel and the little family they had on the ranch, she longed for a sisterly friendship. She really needed to write to Zara soon.

Shaking the hint of sadness from her mind, Yetta concentrated on the fabrics once again. She found a rust red calico fabric with cream and brown flowers she liked; grabbing it and a bolt of white, she stacked them off to the side and turned toward the notions.

Yetta chose her thread and buttons for the dress. Then she grabbed more from her list: white thread, a package of sewing needles, and a cloth measuring tape. She took everything to the counter and unloaded her arms.

Mrs. O'Brien glanced over her shoulder from atop a step stool, a tin container in her hands she'd just retrieved from the top shelf on the wall.

"All set?" she asked as she climbed down.

"Yes, I think so."

Mrs. O'Brien emptied her hands and approached the counter. Lifting the calico fabric, she smiled and held it up in front of Yetta. "Oh, this'll look lovely on ya. How much do ya need?"

"Three yards," Yetta answered. "And one yard of the white, please."

"Very well." Mrs. O'Brien began unrolling the fabric and measuring it against marks on the glossy wood countertop. She reached for her scissors.

"That reminds me," Yetta said, "I didn't see scissors back there."

"Oh yes, I have them behind the counter," Mrs. O'Brien said as she cut and folded the fabric. "I'll add them to your order."

Nathaniel sidled up to Yetta. "Did you get everything you need?"

Yetta nodded. "I think so."

Yetta's Yearning

Mr. O'Brien returned with a box full of supplies and set it on the far end of the long counter. "Did you want all this on your account?" he asked as he pulled out the ledger.

"That won't be necessary," Nathaniel answered. "And please make sure you add Yetta's name to my account."

"Will do, sir." Mr. O'Brien cleared his throat and asked, "Did you still want to keep John and Clara on the account?"

"Yes, I like them to have access to it."

The other women who'd been browsing the store approached the front. Mrs. O'Brien went to greet them.

"Did ya find what ya need?" she asked.

"I did," one of the ladies answered, sliding a hairbrush and a spool of pink ribbon over the counter to Mrs. O'Brien.

Her face lit up. "Is this for Isabelle? She's got a birthday comin' up, doesn't she?"

"Yes, tomorrow. She'll be twelve," the woman answered proudly. "She's been eyeing this ribbon for some time now."

"It'll look lovely in her dark hair. How much would you like?"

"Could I get a half a yard, please?"

"Absolutely." As Mrs. O'Brien moved to measure and cut the ribbon, she said, "Ladies, I'd like you to meet Yetta. She's new in town—just married Nathaniel Price."

"Hello," the lady making a purchase said with a nod. "I'm Helen King, and this is my sister, Harriett Abernathy. Welcome to town."

"Thank you."

"Nice to meet you," Harriett said, moving closer.

"You as well," Yetta replied.

"So you're out at Triple Peak Ranch."

Yetta wasn't sure if she was asking or making a statement. She answered anyway. "Yes."

Harriett perked with enthusiasm, and with a flick of her wrist said, "Well then, we're practically neighbors. Our farm is just this side of Bear Creek Bend. You come on by if you ever need anything. You hear?"

"I appreciate the offer. Thank you."

"Ready?" Nathaniel asked. He stood beside her, holding their box of supplies.

The women said their goodbyes, and Yetta followed Nathaniel out to the wagon. He loaded the box in the back and turned to her, offering a hand up.

She put her hand in his, then hesitated. "I see the church and the boarding house from here. I think I'd like to walk, if that's alright."

He looked down the street. "Are you sure? It's rather far, and I'm headed that way."

"I'm sure," she answered. "In the city, we walked everywhere. I'll be fine."

He seemed uneasy but conceded. "Well, alright then. I'll be at the livery yard just beyond."

Yetta held her head high as she strutted down the boardwalk in front of the buildings and storefronts. She couldn't believe how much her life had changed in such a short amount of time. It wasn't that she'd disliked her life in the city. She had been content with where she was and who she was with. But at the same time, she'd felt trapped. Stuck in a maze made of buildings and stone, never able to see what lay beyond. Or ever meet someone outside her inner circle.

She was happy here. Colorado was beautiful. And it was wide open. Even from the middle of town, she could see the horizon in one direction and the distant mountains in another. Life out here might not have all the conveniences of a big city, but it had so much more to offer. Sure, she'd heard the rumors of the "wild" west, where the people were uncivilized and rules didn't apply. While that may have crossed her mind, she knew you couldn't have adventure without taking some chances. And in this case, taking the chance had paid off.

She passed the barber and her eyes rose to read the sign of the next building. Post Office. Suddenly she slammed into something. Or someone.

She let out a squeak.

A man in a dark suit stood in her path, his back to her.

"I'm so sorry," she said as he turned to face her. "Oh, it's you, Mister…" Her voice trailed off as she tried to remember his name. She'd met him at the boarding house on her wedding night. He was traveling with the hotel builder.

"Blackwell," he answered flatly, readjusting his suit jacket in a jerking manner.

Ava had been right; there was something about this man that just felt off.

Yetta managed a smile. "Yes, nice to see you again, Mr. Blackwell."

His jaw remained clenched. Yetta's gaze wandered uncomfortably to the ground. She noticed a piece of paper at their feet.

"I think you dropped something," she said as she bent.

Mr. Blackwell swiped the page from the ground before she could reach it.

She straightened. "I'm sorry, I didn't mean to—"

"Well, hello there, Mrs. Price," a friendly voice said. It was Mr. Salzman. "How's married life treating you?" It didn't go unnoticed that Mr. Blackwell shoved the paper into his pants pocket as the older man spoke.

Still taken aback by the other man's strange behavior, it

took her a moment to gather her thoughts. "Uh, very well, thank you. And how are the hotel plans coming along?"

He tugged at his lapels and rocked back on his heels. "Good. Good." He had a jolly way about him that eased the tension.

Yetta relaxed, offering him a smile. "That's good to hear. I look forward to seeing the progress." She took a step to the side. "It was nice to see you, but I must be on my way."

Mr. Salzman tipped his hat. "Good day to you."

Yetta responded with a friendly nod. She wanted to walk away, but she could feel Mr. Blackwell's eyes staring into her. It wasn't in her nature to shy away. Show weakness. So she met his stare.

"Mr. Blackwell," she said with a stiff nod. She was nothing if she wasn't cordial.

His features rigid, he narrowed his gaze.

Yetta noticed his hand still tucked in his pocket. While she was curious what had him acting so strangely, she really had no interest in his business.

Chapter Eleven

Mrs. Chandler greeted Yetta at the door. "Hello, Yetta. Come on in. What brings you by today?"

"Hello, Mrs. Chandler." Yetta crossed the threshold and stepped aside as the woman closed the door behind her. "I'm here to see Ava. Is she in?"

"Sure is. Oh, she'll be so happy to see you. That poor girl doesn't get out much—just sits up in that room reading." Mrs. Chandler leaned in and whispered, "I think her father is a little overprotective if you ask me." She straightened, her voice returning to normal. "Why don't you go on up, and I'll put on some tea. Top of the stairs, second door on the right."

"Okay," Yetta answered, surprised she got a word in.

Yetta made her way up the stairs. A long hallway stretched out in front of her with three doors on each side, all closed. She knocked on Ava's.

A soft voiced responded, "Come in."

Yetta opened the door. The room was small and overcrowded. Besides the two beds and a small side table, wooden boxes and trunks lined any available wall space. A makeshift curtain was strung between the beds for privacy, and at one end of the rope, clothes hung from hangers.

Ava sat on the bed reading a book, her back leaning against the wall. At the sight of Yetta, Ava's face brightened.

"Yetta!" She marked her spot, put down the book, and jumped up. Crossing the room in two steps, she threw her arms around her new friend. "Gosh, am I glad to see you."

"I can tell." Yetta laughed at the tight embrace.

Ava released her, stepping back and taking Yetta's hands as if they were long lost friends. Yetta found it endearing. It reminded her of her sisters back home, especially Zara; being roommates, they were the closest.

"Tell me about married life," Ava said. "Are you happy?"

"I truly am."

Ava let out a longing sigh, her eyes dreamy. "I can't wait to get married." Then after a beat, she dropped Yetta's hands and turned away. The dream was over. "But I don't know if Papa will ever let me."

Maybe Mrs. Chandler was right about Ava's father.

"Sorry, I don't have a chair for you." Ava slid the curtain aside and offered Yetta to sit on the bed opposite.

"This is fine," Yetta said, taking a seat on the edge. Her knees practically touched Ava's. She couldn't believe this girl was crammed in the small room with her overbearing father.

Yetta's instinct kicked in. Just like with all the children who had come to the orphanage, she felt protective over her. Felt the need to take her under her wing—even though she wasn't much older.

She tried not to let her disapproval show on her face. "Does your father let you do *anything*? You said you haven't gotten out much."

"He worries about me. My safety."

That really didn't answer Yetta's question. "Was he always like this, or is it just because you're in a new place?"

Ava's eyes shifted down and back. "It seems like we're always in a new place. Surrounded by strangers."

Yetta wasn't sure what to make of that. And she didn't want to pry. "Well, I'm not a stranger," she said with a confident smile. "What if we got out and went for a little walk together?"

Her mouth pulled to the side. "Oh, I don't know."

"Let's ask him," Yetta said. "Where is he now?"

"Most days he's gone from sunup to sundown."

"Well then, maybe he doesn't need to know." Yetta flashed a devilish grin.

The floor outside Ava's room creaked. A moment later they heard a door and movement in the next room. Both women glanced that way.

"That's Mr. Blackwell's room," Ava said quietly.

Yetta met her gaze. "I ran into him by the post office on my way here," she whispered. "I don't like him." Yetta pushed him from her mind. She was here for Ava, and she was going to make the best of it. She stood and held out her hand. "Come on, let's at least get you out of this room. Mrs. Chandler said she was going to put on some tea."

The parlor was a nice improvement over the stuffy room. Yetta started the conversation by asking Ava what she liked to read. It seemed something the two had in common—a love for books. From there the conversation led to teaching, and Yetta shared her excitement for starting a school and how it all came about.

Then Yetta had an idea. "You should teach!"

Ava looked confused.

"Yes! You would make a great teacher," Yetta said. "And if all goes well, I'm going to need help."

Yetta heard Mrs. Chandler talking in the hall. A moment later she led Nathaniel into the parlor. He held his hat in his hands.

"Afternoon, ladies," he said. "Are you having a nice visit?"

Yetta gazed up at him lovingly. Not only was he kind, with a presence that couldn't be denied, he was also easy on the eyes.

"We are," she answered and looked to Ava, who nodded in agreement.

Mrs. Chandler spoke up. "Would you like some tea, Nathaniel?"

"Thank you, kindly, but Yetta and I will have to be heading back now."

Ava let out a moan of disapproval. "So soon?"

"I'll visit again soon. I promise." Yetta placed her hand over Ava's and flashed her a knowing look. "Please think about our conversation."

ONCE OUT THE DOOR, Nathaniel asked, "So, what was that about? It seemed serious."

"I told Ava I thought she would make a good teacher and that I'm probably going to need help," Yetta answered.

They approached the wagon, parked at the foot of the boarding house steps. Nathaniel held out a hand for Yetta. "And she's not interested?"

"I think she is." Yetta put her hand in Nathaniel's and glanced back at the house. Ava watched from the window. Yetta tossed her a smile and turned back. "But I don't know if her father will allow it."

Nathaniel helped Yetta into the wagon, and they continued their conversation on the ride home. Yetta voiced her concern for Ava, and her need to help the young woman flourish if she was ever going to get out from under her father's thumb.

There was that determination again. Nathaniel had the feeling that if his wife was passionate about something, there was no backing down. He hoped it didn't get her in trouble someday.

When they arrived back at the homestead, Nathaniel stopped in front of the house. He helped Yetta down and unloaded the supplies from the back, Harley at his feet the whole time. But then, instead of going inside, Yetta insisted on accompanying Nathaniel on to the barn.

"I have so much to learn," she said. "I want to watch how you unhitch the horses. I also want to learn how to put a saddle on and ride a horse."

Nathaniel smiled at her enthusiasm. She was unlike any woman he'd met before. The last time he'd courted had been back in Texas. It was a meeting arranged by the families, both of wealth and stature. It had gone on for about a month, but she was awful. A spoiled brat. She wouldn't do a thing for herself, let alone others.

Inside the barn, Jacob greeted them. Grabbing ahold of one of the harnesses and taking control, he said, "I'll take care of them, Mr. Price."

"That's alright, Jacob. I've got it today," he said. "Yetta would like to learn."

Jacob flashed Yetta a smile. "Is that so, ma'am?"

"It is." Yetta approached the mare looking out from a nearby stall and rubbed behind her ear. "I also want to learn how to saddle and ride a horse."

"I was thinking after we put away the team, we could saddle up a couple of horses and ride out to check on the cattle in the upper pasture," Nathaniel said.

Yetta beamed with excitement. "Really? We could do that today?"

"Sure."

Though Yetta was the teacher, Nathaniel enjoyed playing the part as he unhitched the horses from the neck yoke and removed their harnesses. He explained what each thing was and its use.

He did the same when they saddled the horses, even explaining that different horses were used for different jobs. He was impressed with how quickly she caught on. Her only disadvantage at this point was her lack of strength. Still, she managed.

He chose Athena for Yetta's first ride. She was on the smaller side and easy-going.

"Steady, Athena," he purred, ready to help Yetta into the saddle.

"Athena?" Yetta repeated in surprise.

"Yes, like the Greek goddess," he said.

"I know who she is." Yetta beamed. "I just didn't know that you were familiar with Greek mythology."

"I find it fascinating," he said, giving Yetta a boost up.

He passed her the reins and kept one hand on Athena while he went over some basic instructions with Yetta: first how to properly hold the reins, then how to move them.

"Slight movements is all it takes with her," he warned. "And to make her go, just give a little tap with your legs."

Stroking Athena's mane, Yetta smiled big. "Okay."

Nathaniel chuckled. "Are you listening?"

"Yes," she answered. "Slight movements. Little tap. Can we go now?"

Nathaniel smiled. He loved her fun, adventurous spirit.

Chapter Twelve

Yetta couldn't stop smiling. Riding through the open meadow with the wind in her hair was the most amazing feeling. She felt tall and invincible sitting atop Athena.

Yetta stroked Athena's golden mane. "I can't wait to tell Zara about you," she whispered. Then she glanced over at Nathaniel, riding beside her. *And about you.* She knew Zara would be thrilled to know that her husband liked Greek mythology.

Yetta tapped the horse again, wanting to go faster.

"Hey!" Nathaniel called out from behind.

Yetta giggled.

He caught up to her, and she slowed.

"You're doing great," he said. "You're a natural."

They rode side by side for several more minutes.

"There's the herd, up ahead." Nathaniel pointed.

Yetta had been at Triple Peak for almost a week, and she had yet to see the cattle—Nathaniel had called them longhorns. And from this distance, she still didn't have a good view. They just looked like a dark mass on the horizon.

When they got up close, Yetta realized why they were called longhorns. Her jaw dropped at the impressive sight.

"They're amazing." Yetta held Athena back, letting Nathaniel take the lead as they strolled up to the herd. "Do we have to do anything with them?"

"Nope," he answered. "I'm just getting a rough count and checking to be sure that nothing looks out of the ordinary. No injuries, that sort of thing."

"How many do you have?"

"Altogether, about a thousand head," he replied. "In this group, about four-fifty."

"Where are the rest?" She worried she was asking too many questions.

"Back the other way, in the lower pasture."

"Can we go check on them too?" She was enjoying herself too much—wasn't ready to go back.

"Uhh," he hummed, glancing at the sun in the sky. "I guess we'd have time for that."

A few minutes later, Nathaniel had come to what seemed to be the last few cattle.

"All looks good here," he said. He tugged the reins to the side, and his horse made a wide turn. "We can head out."

Nathaniel couldn't remember ever going on a casual ride with a woman. He loved how Yetta was opening him up to new things and wondered what other surprises she had in store for him.

They came to the crest, overlooking the cattle in the valley of what Nathaniel referred to as the lower pasture. There was no need to make the trek down the hill; all seemed well from his vantage point.

Yetta's Yearning

He took a deep, refreshing breath. This was his favorite time of the day—late afternoon—when the day was winding down.

"Sun's about to touch the mountains," he declared, his voice low as to not disturb the peaceful silence.

Yetta matched his soft tone. "I've never seen such a brilliant orange."

They sat in their saddles, quietly watching the sunset, before heading back.

With the homestead in sight, Nathaniel said, "Well, I don't know about you, but I'm famished."

"I'll whip something up fast as I can." Yetta was quiet a moment, then asked, "What's that sound?"

Nathaniel held a hand out, motioning to stop so he could listen. He heard the familiar *ch-ch-ch* of a rattler. "Rattlesnake," he said, scanning their surroundings.

"Where is it?" her voice came out in squeak.

"There." Nathaniel pointed a couple yards away from Athena. "Don't move—"

But it was too late.

Yetta let out a scream and gave Athena a kick.

The horse took two steps, almost stepping on the snake, before realizing it was there. Suddenly spooked, Athena reared up, dumping Yetta to the ground.

"Yetta!" Nathaniel cried, dismounting his horse in a rush as the snake slithered off in one direction and Athena in another. He knelt by Yetta's side. "Are you all right? Are you hurt?"

She blinked up at him, looking dazed. "I think so."

He helped her sit up. "Are you sure?"

"Yeah." Yetta rubbed the back of her head, then perked up with wide eyes. "Where's the rattlesnake? Is Athena okay?"

Nathaniel let out an exasperated breath and collapsed his legs, landing on his rump beside her. "You're worried about the horse?" he snorted. "Woman! You coulda been killed."

Chapter Thirteen

Yetta had been looking forward to this day all week—the day they'd go back to the camp at Nolan Gulch and meet with the families about starting the school. So, when Nathaniel noticed the dark clouds on the horizon, the last thing he wanted to do was cancel.

With the team hitched and ready to go, he went to find Yetta.

She was at the desk in the parlor gathering her things.

"I'd like to head out right away," he said. "It looks like we might have bad weather moving in later today. We'll have to make this a quick trip."

Minutes later they were on their way. The gloomy sky made for an ominous ride into the mountains.

As the camp came into view, they noticed a few men saddling up horses. Nathaniel recognized three out of the four.

"That's odd," he muttered.

He pulled the wagon up close and stopped. While the men seemed glad to see him, concern weighed heavy on their expressions.

"What's going on?" Nathaniel asked.

"We're roundin' up a search party," Jeb Cromwell said as he approached.

"For what? Can I assist in any way?"

Jeb rubbed the back of his neck. Looking up at Nathaniel, he said, "It's Sebastian. He hasn't returned for three days."

Nathaniel flashed a look to Yetta, concern tight in his chest.

Her eyes held the same concern. "Go."

He grimaced. "But how can I leave you?"

"Right now, your friend needs you more," she urged and reached for the reins.

Torn, Nathaniel's lips pursed as he held her gaze. Finally, he let out a noisy huff and turned back to Jeb. "Got a horse I can borrow?"

Jeb gave a nod and hollered to his crew, "We've got one more. Saddle up another horse."

Nathaniel grabbed Yetta's face in both hands and planted a hard kiss on her lips. He pulled his lips away but held her close, staring intensely into her eyes. "Don't stay long. I don't want you caught out in this storm alone."

"Okay," she answered.

"Let Simpson know what's going on. And don't forget, Jacob is there, he'll unhitch the horses and help with anything else you need. I don't know when I'll be back," he spoke hurriedly.

"I know," Yetta replied. "I'll be okay."

"I love you, Yetta Price."

He kissed her again and swiftly hopped out of the wagon.

Nathaniel could already feel it in his leg. The ache that told him the bad weather was moving in fast. With the horses ready to go, the party of five took off. They headed north, toward Sebastian's last known whereabouts. Although, an exact location wasn't known. That was typical in this business to keep claims safe from thieves.

For almost an hour, they rode, only slowing when they came to a junction. They had three choices: follow the trail toward the summit, cut left toward the river, or veer right and head into rockier terrain.

While the other four men discussed their options, Nathaniel was deep in thought. This area seemed familiar to him. Tugging at the reins, his horse shuffled to the side and back and forth as Nathaniel inspected his surroundings.

He heard Henry say, "Y'all head toward the river. We'll take the summit." He referred to himself and his brother, William.

"Vat about zis vay?" the other man asked with a thick German accent, pointing toward the rockier terrain.

"Nobody'd go that way, Dieter. It's too narrow and rocky. Just too dangerous." As William said the words, Nathaniel remembered saying the same thing about two years ago when Sebastian wanted to explore that direction.

"But that's just what he did!" Nathaniel said in a rush, leaning forward in his seat and giving his horse a kick.

SEEING Nathaniel ride away without her terrified Yetta, though she'd never let on. She grabbed the carpet bag and jumped down from the wagon, determined to continue with her business.

A boy of about ten stood in front of her when she turned around.

"You Mrs. Price?" he asked.

Yetta recognized a teaching moment. "The correct phrasing is '*are you* Mrs. Price?'"

Wide eyed, the boy repeated, "Are you Mrs. Price?"

Yetta smiled. "Very good. And yes I am."

"My momma told me t' bring ya t' the meetin'."

The boy scampered off ahead, and Yetta followed. He directed her to a larger tent—the one she assumed they'd mentioned before as a place for gatherings—and slipped inside. Yetta pushed the flap aside and stopped in her tracks. Inside was a sea of people. Rows and rows of parents sitting on wooden benches.

Mrs. Jennings rushed to Yetta's side. "I'm so glad you made the trip. I was worried the weather would scare ya off."

"Nope, I wouldn't miss it," Yetta replied, still in shock.

"Someone said they saw Nathaniel go out with the search party, so we'll try to keep this short to get you on your way before the rain starts."

"Great." Yetta looked around. "I can't believe the crowd."

"They're all looking forward to meeting you and hearing what you have to say." Mrs. Jennings led Yetta to the front and called out above the din, "Okay, everyone, let's get started."

The crowd quieted.

Yetta hesitated. She'd never spoken in front of such a large crowd. Mrs. Jennings threw her an encouraging look.

"Hello, I'm Ye—" she stuttered and corrected, "Mrs. Price. I taught at the Wigg School in New York City and have been given the opportunity to continue Madam Wigg's teachings here in Colorado…"

Yetta kept the conversation brief, laying out her goals, and then taking questions. She was delighted by the response. In fact, when one father began to gripe, the crowd reacted, and he backed off. As a whole, they came to an agreement on a small initial fee to order some books and supplies. They also agreed on waiting until September to start. Which wasn't that far off.

Nearly a half hour had passed when Mrs. Jennings called the meeting to an end and sent Yetta on her way.

At first it felt strange, leaving the camp and heading home alone. Then she reminded herself that in just a few weeks' time, she would be making the trek back and forth by herself every day. She couldn't possibly expect Nathaniel to escort her everywhere. The thought seemed to ease her mind a bit. Until she remembered that he wouldn't be waiting for her at home.

Yetta made it all the way to the outskirts of Triple Peak Ranch before the first drops of rain started to fall. They began slow and fat, and were somewhat refreshing.

With a good hundred yards to go, Harley greeted the wagon. She fell in step with the horses as if she now led the way. Yetta smiled. The shepherd managed to ease the loneliness that loomed.

Harley let out a bark, and a moment later Jacob opened the barn doors, just in time for Yetta to guide the team inside and get out of the rain. Pulling to a stop, Yetta engaged the brake.

"Where's Mr. Price?" Jacob went to work unhitching the team from the yoke.

Yetta hopped down from the wagon. "His help was needed. It seems his friend is missing, so they sent out a search party."

Jacob stopped and met her gaze, his brow knitted. "Oh. I'm sorry to hear that. Uh…you go on ahead, ma'am. I'll take care of things here."

"Thank you. I need to let Simpson know what's going

on." Yetta grabbed her bag out of the wagon. "Do you know where I can find him?"

"Uh, yeah, he just went inside seeing as how the rain was startin'."

Yetta took off for the cabin. The drops were still thick and scattered, so she shielded herself with her carpet bag, holding it above her head with two hands.

She knocked twice on the cabin door. "It's Yetta," she called out.

Clara opened the door in a rush. "Get in out of the rain! You know you don't have to knock," she scolded.

Yetta stepped inside, lowered her bag, and brushed herself off. Clara grabbed a tea towel from the kitchen counter and handed it to Yetta.

Simpson watched from a seat at the kitchen table, a mug in front of him. "Everything all right?"

Before she could answer, Clara chimed in again. "What are you doing out there anyway? It's gonna start pourin' any minute."

Yetta let out a breath, calming herself from the short run. She dabbed her face with the towel. "I just came to tell you that Nathaniel's friend, Sebastian Carter, is missing."

Simpson stood. "What's that you say?"

"When we got to the camp at Nolan Gulch, they were putting together a search party to go looking for him. Apparently, he hadn't returned to camp in three days." She paused, taking a breath. "Nathaniel went with them."

A groan rumbled deep in Simpson's throat, and his brows hovered over brooding eyes. "I gotta bad feelin' 'bout this."

Yetta's eyes widened. She was already worried. "Why do you say that?"

The older man walked to the window at the back. It

faced the mountains. Looking out, he shook his head. "We just don't know what this storm is gonna do. This time of year, they can be brutal. Flooding, landslides…" Holding up his balled hand, he met her gaze and added, "Hail the size of my fist."

Chapter Fourteen

The rain came down so hard and fast that Nathaniel could hardly see his own hand in front of his face. It was slow going, and as much as he wanted to continue, he knew they'd have to find shelter and wait out the storm.

Around the next bend, he spotted what seemed to be an opening in the rock face.

"Wait here!" Nathaniel hollered through the clamor of the rainfall to the men behind him.

He slid off his horse, landing on two feet in the slippery mud, and carefully made his way to the opening. Though dark, it looked like there'd be enough room for five men.

"Hello!"

He turned his ear and listened for an echo.

Hello. Hello. Hello.

He was pleased with the response. It told him the cave went farther back than he could see.

They secured the horses close to the opening where there was a bit of an overhang, then moved farther inside and hunkered down. After a few minutes their eyes adjusted to the dark, and the men, who were wet and cold, began scrounging for dry wood or anything they could burn.

William had a fire going in no time. He was down on one knee in front of it while the other men stood around. "I sure hope you're right about this," he griped as he poked at the fire with a stick, sending embers into the air.

Nathaniel knew what he was talking about. And he *was* sure of it. Just like he was sure that if it hadn't been for the rain, they would have found Sebastian's trail already.

The look on Henry's face matched William's. It was clear the brothers had their doubts.

Jeb rubbed his hands together and held them above the flame. "Nathaniel knows Sebastian better than anyone else. If *he* thinks he went this way, then I trust him."

Nathaniel's mouth pulled to one side, and he gave a mindful nod, grateful for Jeb's faith in him.

Without another word about it, the men settled in for the wait. Minutes turned to hours, day turned to night, and there was less talk as one by one the men gave in to sleep.

"Looks like ve're here till mornink," Dieter mumbled just before he began snoring.

That left Nathaniel alone with his thoughts. He wandered to the front of the cave and peered into the night, worried they would be too late. He shook his head, refusing to think like that. He owed Sebastian his life and couldn't let him down.

Nathaniel recalled the cave-in five years ago. If it wasn't for Sebastian, he would be dead. He was reminded of it every time the weather changed.

He bent and mindlessly rubbed his left leg, just below the knee. It ached something awful.

It was still so vivid in his mind, lying pinned under the heavy beam as the rock above him continued to crumble. He should've died that day—he'd already made peace with it. So, when he saw the ball of light floating through the dust-filled tunnel, moving ever closer, he thought the angels had come for him.

He remembered closing his eyes, preparing for his eternal slumber. And the hand touching his shoulder. And then the voice…

"Nathaniel…"

It was Sebastian. He had fought his way through the rubble—put his own life in danger—and with a strength Nathaniel couldn't explain, pulled him to safety.

Nathaniel blinked away visions of the past. Back in the here and now, it seemed as though the rain was letting up. He stepped outside to assess the situation and realized the visibility was actually quite good. Good enough to continue his search, he decided.

He untethered his ride and left the shelter of the cave. This time on foot, guiding the horse by the reins. He walked until first light, then mounted once again.

While the rain had finally stopped, it would've washed away any tracks. He kept his eyes peeled for other clues that someone had come through in the last few days. That could be in the form of broken branches, brush tamped down, or human litter of any kind.

But as it turned out, the best clue would be impossible to miss.

Standing near a tree, in a small grassy area was Sebastian's horse, Dolly. He'd recognize the dappled mare anywhere.

From atop his own horse, Nathaniel scanned the area.

"Sebastian!"

He silently waited.

"Sebastian Carter!"

Again nothing.

He dismounted and approached Dolly as she grazed.

"Why aren't you tied up?" he asked, giving her the once over.

Nathaniel had a bad feeling about this.

THE SOUND of a door woke Yetta, and her head snapped up from the table where she'd fallen asleep. "Nathaniel?"

"It's just me," Clara answered from across the dimly lit kitchen. The only light came from a lamp by the front door. "I'm sorry, I didn't mean to wake you."

Yetta rubbed her aching neck. "How long was I sleeping?"

"Almost an hour."

With knitted brow, Yetta glanced around the room and out into the center hall. "Where are Simpson and Jacob?" she asked.

They had all joined Yetta in the big house to wait out the storm. Even Harley, who normally didn't come inside, was sprawled out on the kitchen floor.

Clara shot an uneasy look at Yetta. "They went to check on the cattle."

"What!" Yetta shot to her feet, shoulders tensed, eyes wide. "When? Why didn't they wake me? I would've gone with them."

Clara's mouth quirked. She put a hand on Yetta's arm. "Because you were exhausted, and they knew you would insist on going with them—"

"But as Nathaniel's wife, the cattle—the business—are my responsibility." She walked to the window and peered out into the darkness. "What if something happens to them?"

"They've got this, sweetie. This is what they do. It's their life." Clara turned and crossed to the pantry. "You know what I do when I'm worried…I bake," she said as she grabbed the sack of flour.

The front door burst open and banged against the interior wall. Startled, the women locked eyes.

"Help." Jacob's voice sounded labored.

The flour fell from Clara's grasp, hitting the floor and exploding as she and Yetta ran out of the room.

Jacob stood at the threshold, holding Simpson's arm, which was wrapped around his shoulders. Jacob's other hand held the older man at the waist. Simpson looked weak, his knees partially bent and head rolling forward. Behind them, the unrelenting rain continued.

"John!" Clara cried and ran to him.

The older man huffed a breath through his teeth.

"What happened?" Yetta moved to Simpson's other side.

"We were trying to move the herd out of the valley, and he started having chest pains," Jacob answered as they moved Simpson into the parlor.

Clara rushed around, grabbing blankets and returning to her husband's side. She ripped the wet jacket and shirt off his body, wrapped a blanket around his shoulders, then stuffed a pillow under his head as they eased him onto the sofa.

"I just need to lay down for a while and I'll be fine," Simpson groaned. "I need to get back out there."

"You're not leaving this sofa!" Clara spat.

Yetta saw the concern on Jacob's face as he ran his hands through his hair. But it seemed there was more on his mind than the older man's health.

Yetta gave a nod to the side, beckoning Jacob into the other room. He followed.

"What's going on? Why are you moving the herd?" She kept her voice low as to not agitate Simpson any further.

Jacob's lip twitched, and his nose wrinkled. "The creek is really high, and I'm afraid the valley is going to flood. I've got to get the cattle out of there."

"Can that really happen? I mean, the rain has got to be ending soon. Wouldn't it have already flooded by now?"

Jacob shook his head, a dire look on his face. "Run-off from the mountains hasn't hit us yet. We could have just a few hours to get them out of there or else…" His voice trailed off.

"Or else what?" she prodded.

He glanced over his shoulder to be sure Simpson and Clara weren't listening. "They'll drown. Wash away," he whispered.

Yetta's chest felt heavy. She couldn't let everything Nathaniel had worked for be washed away. She looked down at the dress she was wearing.

This won't do, she thought and took off up the stairs.

Less than two minutes later she returned, wearing Nathaniel's shirt and trousers. His clothes hung off her small frame, and she had to use one of his belts tied in a knot to keep the trousers from falling to the floor.

Jacob's brow rose at the sight of her as she marched past.

"Clara, I have to borrow your shoes and coat," she said, her voice sounded strong and demanding, even to her.

She pulled on the older woman's work shoes and grabbed her coat off the hook by the door. As she slipped the coat on, Clara appeared in the doorway. Yetta expected an argument from her.

"Be safe."

Yetta was taken aback. But grateful.

"We will." She turned to Jacob. "Let's go."

Chapter Fifteen

"Sebastian!" Nathaniel called his name again and again as he combed the area around where he'd found Dolly. And the only prints he saw in the mud were from her.

He heard the clomping of hooves coming up the trail, the others catching up.

A moment later, they rounded the bend and caught sight of Nathaniel and *two* horses.

"Is that Dolly?" one asked.

"Yep," Nathaniel answered. "No sign of Sebastian, though."

Jeb scanned the horizon. "I'll head up the trail a ways and see if there's any trace of activity," he said and continued on.

The other men hopped off their horses, and together, they widened their search.

Nathaniel left the area of the natural path and scaled up the side of the hill. He was looking for caves or crevices that Sebastian might've sought shelter in. Or at the very least, he'd get a better view from up high.

"Over here!" William hollered.

Yetta's Yearning

Everyone went running.

William stood at the edge, near a steep drop off. He pointed down to a spot just in front of his feet where it looked as though the ground had given way—like someone had stepped too close.

Then something caught Nathaniel's attention at the bottom, a good thirty feet below. He couldn't tell what exactly it was other than it was white.

Minding his own footing, he followed the ridgeline as he peered below. While he hoped they'd found his friend, he worried they'd be taking home a body.

"What is that?" Jeb muttered to no one in particular.

Finally, Nathaniel could see that it was a piece of white cloth tied around a rock.

It was a marker.

A sign.

Adrenalin pumping, Nathaniel launched himself over the side and down the incline in a controlled slide.

"Grab the rope out of the packs!" Jeb shouted to the others.

Nathaniel reached the bottom and ran over to the marker. He picked it up and examined it. The cloth looked to be torn from the bottom hem of a shirt, and it was stained with bloody fingerprints.

"Sebastian!" he called again, letting the cloth-wrapped rock fall to the ground.

His head snapped to the top of the ridge where Sebastian may have fallen from. Then his eyes traced a path toward the bottom as his mind worked out logical scenarios.

He could've sworn he heard something.

"Do you see—" Jeb started to say, but Nathaniel held a hand up to quiet him.

Nathaniel stood still, listening intently.

There it was again, albeit faint. *Clack-clack-clack. Clack. Clack. Clack. Clack-clack-clack.*

"SOS!" Nathaniel yelled in surprise.

He followed the sound, which took him closer to the base of the hillside. He looked in and around the rock and brush.

Clack-clack-clack. Louder this time. *Clack. Clack. Clack.* He was getting closer.

"Sebastian, where are you?"

Clack-clack-clack.

Nathaniel took another step along the base, and the sound stopped.

After a beat, he heard the raspy whisper, "Down here."

Nathaniel's gaze dropped just as a hand reached out from under a rocky overhang. He dropped to one knee, and with one hand on the rock face, he crouched.

There lay Sebastian, propped slightly, in the small space that was maybe two and a half feet high. One leg was splinted with wood and wrapped with strips of cloth, similar to the one tied to the rock. He held one arm close to his body, cradling his side.

"Boy am I glad to see you." Sebastian strained to speak. Nathaniel could see it on his face and in the way his arm tensed around his side. It told him that in addition to the obvious broken leg, his friend also had broken ribs.

"I was going to say the same thing," Nathaniel replied with a smile.

Groaning in pain, Sebastian tried to move toward the edge of the opening.

Nathaniel held up a hand. "Don't move. We'll get you out of there."

He stood and moved back into the open area to report to the others waiting at the top of the ridge. "He's down here! We're going to need a stretcher to transport him."

Yetta's Yearning

"Okay, we're working on it," Jeb said. Then he added, "Henry thinks he found an easier way for you to get out of there. It's back that way." He pointed in the direction they'd come up the path.

"Did ya hear that?" Nathaniel called to Sebastian. "We'll have you out of here in no time."

YETTA COULDN'T THINK of a time she'd been colder or wetter. The rain was letting up, but daybreak was still almost an hour away. Even if the rain stopped now, there'd be no sun to warm her. She tried not to think about it, instead keeping her mind busy praying for everyone's safety.

This was only her second time on a horse. And her ability to control it was a matter of life or death. This one was a little more finicky than Athena.

The herd huddled close together in the storm. Jacob managed to maneuver them to face the direction he wanted. He told Yetta his plan was to push them a few hundred yards downstream, then drive them to the left, up an embankment and out of the valley, to higher ground. Normally they drove them downstream much farther, where the incline was gradual.

He directed her to the right of the herd, up toward the front.

"Keep a steady pace; they should follow. I'll move 'em from behind," he said. "Listen for my whistle"—he demonstrated—"that'll be my signal to start pushing toward the left and up the hill."

"Okay," she answered. She understood his instructions. How to carry them out was a different story.

Jacob looked down to Nathaniel's trusty shepherd standing nearby. "Harley will help you."

The shepherd's gaze met Jacob's. He clicked his tongue and waved his arm forward, the universal gesture for "onward."

And just like that, it was as if the shepherd knew she had a job to do. Her ears went up and her eyes forward. Suddenly Yetta felt more at ease. She knew Harley wouldn't let her down.

Moving the herd was slow-going. But at least the rain had stopped and the darkness was already on its way out.

Finally, Yetta heard the whistle. She tugged the reins to the left, steering her horse closer to the herd, and Harley followed suit. The cattle began moving left.

Yetta smiled. She couldn't believe it was working—that *she* was actually driving the cattle like a real cowboy. *Oh, if my sisters could see me now,* she thought.

They took the hill at an angle to make it easier on the cattle. Yetta loved watching Harley at work. She seemed to smile as she trotted alongside the front line. And when one tried to stray, Harley got them back in line.

Yetta reached the crest and stopped to look back. What a sight. Over five-hundred head of cattle filled the hillside and stretched back at least twice as far. She noticed that as the hill got muddier and trampled, the cattle began to slow. Some tried to break the line at the turning point, and Jacob rode faster to cut them off. Once they were back in line, he circled around and returned to the rear, urging them forward.

Woof. Harley had doubled back to check on Yetta.

Yetta's gaze went back to that turning point. The cattle kept wanting to continue forward in the basin instead of going left up the incline. Jacob needed help.

Yetta turned back to Harley. She clicked her tongue as Jacob had and gave the "onward" gesture. She needed

Yetta's Yearning

Harley to keep the herd going forward, because Yetta was going back down the hill.

Pulling the reins around and giving a kick, Yetta's ride took off. A little faster than she expected. She held on tight, reaching the valley floor in less than half the time it took to get to the top.

It took some maneuvering, zig-zagging, and trial and error, but eventually she got the stragglers turned around. She sat up in the saddle and looked back to find Jacob. She was surprised at how close they were to having the last of the herd start making the turn to go up the hill.

Jacob's gaze met Yetta's. He smiled and waved.

Facing forward and relaxing in her seat, Yetta smiled proudly and joined the pace of the herd once again. And as she felt the sun warm her face, she had a feeling everything was going to be okay. She just hoped Nathaniel was having good luck as well.

Yetta's gaze wandered to the stream to her right. She could tell it had risen just in the time it had taken her to lead the cattle to the top and come back down.

Her eyes narrowed as she stared a moment. She would swear it was rising right in front of her eyes. She pulled the reins to the right and circled back, riding alongside the flowing water. It was so hard to tell. Were her eyes playing games with her? She *was* exhausted, after all.

She spotted the tip of a large rock sticking out along the bank and stopped to watch. In the matter of four heartbeats, the rock disappeared. At this rate the water would breach the bank in just a few minutes.

"Jacob!" she cried, pointing to the rising water.

He got one look and his head snapped in the other direction, just as they heard a mighty roar.

The valley was about to flood.

Chapter Sixteen

The clear skies made the trip back down the mountain much easier for Nathaniel and the others. Even though they were taking it slow with the extra cargo, they were making good time.

The brothers led the group, ensuring a clear path.

Jeb was next in line. He pulled Sebastian in a makeshift stretcher, made of branches and strung together with rope. It was attached to his horse, and it dragged along the path behind them.

While Sebastian didn't seem to be lucid, each bump sent him moaning in pain.

Nathaniel followed behind with Sebastian's horse, Dolly, in tow, and Dieter took up the rear.

After more than an hour, Nathaniel was grateful to be off the rockier terrain and back onto the smoother, more usable path.

As they got closer to camp, Jeb sent Dieter on ahead to ready a wagon to transport Sebastian into town.

"We'll have ya to Doc Miller's soon," Nathaniel said, trying to ease his friend's mind. Or maybe he was trying to ease his own, since he couldn't be sure his friend was truly hearing anything they said.

Pulling into camp, they were met with a small crowd, all happy to see Sebastian Carter had been found. Thanks to Dieter, they had a wagon hitched and ready to go, the back piled with blankets for comfort.

The scene warmed Nathaniel's heart. These were good people, who took care of their own.

With plenty of help, they had Sebastian transferred to the wagon in no time.

Only Nathaniel and Jeb continued on to town.

Fifteen minutes later, the wagon pulled up in front of Doc Miller's, and Nathaniel hopped out. He rushed up to the door and flung it open.

"Hey, Doc! Are ya here?" he called out.

The place was quiet.

With his hand still on the door handle, something caught his attention on the glass. A small piece of paper with bold print: AT BOARDING HOUSE.

Nathaniel pulled the door shut and ran across the street to the Chandler Boarding House. He rushed through the door.

He called out once again, "I'm looking for Doc! Is he here?"

Both Doc Miller and Mrs. Chandler hurried to greet him at the door.

"What is it?" Doc asked.

"It's Sebastian," Nathaniel replied. "He's taken a bad fall. Got a broken leg and at least a few broken ribs, I'd guess."

Doc flashed a glance to Mrs. Chandler.

"Bring him in here," she said. "I've got an extra room

we can put him in."

While Nathaniel went to get Jeb and bring Sebastian into the boarding house, the doc went to fetch his medical bag and supplies.

Jeb pulled the wagon as close to the steps as he could.

"Sebastian," Nathaniel said, trying to stir him. "We're going to move you inside now."

His friend opened his eyes and nodded.

Nathaniel and Jeb carried him in a sitting position with a basket made by linking their arms. Sebastian managed to hold on by wrapping one arm around one of their necks. His other arm remained at his side, protecting his ribs.

Mrs. Chandler stood at the doorway and directed them as they entered.

"I've got a room down here we'll put him in," she said. "Right this way."

They followed her around the corner to a small room and gently laid him on the bed. She'd already removed the top blankets.

"This'll be good," she added. "I can keep a better eye on him down here." This wasn't the first time her boarding house had been used for the critically ill or injured.

The men stepped back and let the older woman take over. She removed the splint from his leg and began tearing his clothes off gently, methodically, causing little stress to the patient. Then she covered him with a sheet.

Doc Miller entered in the room and went to the other side of the bed. He set his medical bag on a chair in the corner.

"How did this happen?" he asked of the other men.

"We found him north of Ute Pass. It looks like he fell about thirty feet," Nathaniel said. "He'd been missing three days."

Yetta's Yearning

Ava stepped in the doorway. "Here's the warm water and towels you asked for, ma'am."

"Thanks, dear," Mrs. Chandler replied.

Ava set them on the side table. "What else can I do to help?"

"There's a pot of soup on the stove. Could you bring a bowl of the broth? We'll see if we can get some nourishment in him."

"Yes, ma'am."

The doc held a stethoscope to Sebastian's chest and the room quieted. After moving it to several spots and listening, he said, "His breathing is shallow on the right side."

"What does that mean?" Jeb asked.

The doc ran his fingers along each of Sebastian's ribs, starting from the top. The farther down he went, the more Sebastian cringed. Then the doc hit a particularly tender spot and Sebastian yelped.

"Yep, definitely from the broken ribs," Doc Miller said. "The good news is that I don't hear any gurgling that would indicate internal bleeding."

Then the doc moved down to tend to the broken leg. He lifted the sheet. With just a glance he said, "I'm going to need to set that. But first we'll need to clean him up. Looks like part of the bone poked through the skin."

Nathaniel's stomach turned. "Do you think he's going to be okay, Doc?"

"With a lot of rest," he answered with a nod.

"He can stay here as long as it takes," Mrs. Chandler said.

"Thank you, Mrs. Chandler," Nathaniel said. "And once he's well enough to be moved, he can come stay with me and Yetta until he's back on his feet."

Good heavens, Yetta.

He turned toward Jeb. "I have to go!"

Chapter Seventeen

Yetta froze in panic.

What was she to do? Keep moving the herd or run for the hills?

Maybe there was still time to save them. There were only about twenty head left in the basin.

"Go! Get outta here!" Jacob shouted.

"I'm not leaving until we get them all out!" she shouted back.

Jacob scowled and groaned in frustration. Then he yanked a rifle from its holder attached to his saddle, cocked the hammer, pointed it straight up, and pulled the trigger, launching a stampede. The rumble of the fleeing cattle blended with the roar of the water, and above that, the echo of the gunshot bounced off the valley walls.

Yetta gave a kick and her ride joined the rush of the stampede. As she started up the side of the hill, she looked back to check that Jacob was right behind her.

He was still in the basin.

And not far behind him, a wall of water followed.

She waved her arms. "Look out!"

But there was no chance of being heard over everything else.

Yetta's heart pounded violently in her chest. She had to get his attention—and fast.

She looked down at the rifle tucked in her own saddle. She'd never held a gun before, let alone fired one. But she'd just watched Jacob fire off a shot, and it looked like there wasn't much to it.

Without another thought, Yetta pulled the rifle free. It was heavier than she expected. She cocked the hammer. Then holding on with both hands, she pointed it upwards and fired.

The kickback surprised her and nearly knocked her off her horse. She struggled to keep hold of the weapon and steady herself in the saddle at the same time, all the while knowing she had to get out of there or she too could be swept away.

Suddenly, Jacob was there beside her. And in one swift move he grabbed the rifle with one hand and slapped her horse on the backside with the other.

Yetta tucked her body in close. Gripping the saddle horn with both hands, she held on for dear life.

In a matter of seconds, the water rushed by behind them.

When they reached the crest, Yetta grabbed the reins and slowed to a stop.

Jacob rode up beside her. "Are you all right?"

Speechless, Yetta gave a nod.

Everything was so quiet and peaceful now.

In front of her, the herd was calming—some grazed in the distance. She turned in her seat and looked out to the valley below. The entire basin was covered with water; it too looked calm.

Yetta's pulse continued to race; it was hard to breathe.

But she had to know.

"Did we save everyone?" she asked.

Jacob nodded. "*You* saved everyone…including *me*," he answered, raising his brow.

The ride back to the homestead was quiet. Yetta and Jacob took their time, needing a well-deserved breather from the excitement. Her body ached. She felt as though she could sleep for days.

Even Harley seemed spent.

While she was proud of what she'd accomplished in the early morning hours, the reality of the danger she'd just endured weighed heavy on her mind.

She began to question her decisions.

Maybe she wasn't cut out for this kind of life.

The mishap with the Death Lilies came to mind. So did the incident with the rattlesnake that ended with her falling off a horse. It seemed everything in Colorado wanted to kill her.

A dread came over her, and suddenly, Yetta wanted to go back to New York City. Back to the safety of the Wigg School and Foundling Home. Maybe if she left soon, she'd get there before Wiggie succumbed to her illness.

With her mind made up and her heart broken, Yetta hopped off her horse and followed Jacob and Harley on foot the last hundred yards or so. As they got closer to the barn, the shepherd's ears perked up, and she let out an excited bark.

Yetta wasn't sure why…until the barn doors opened, and Nathaniel stepped out.

One look at him and Yetta knew it was all worth it. That she'd do it all again tomorrow, just to be with Nathaniel.

Yetta's Yearning

Yetta's breath caught in her throat, and the tears she'd been holding broke free. She released the reins and rushed to Nathaniel.

Nathaniel met her halfway as they rushed into each other's arms. Holding her tight, he swept her off her feet, and they swung in a circle with the momentum.

As they came to rest, her feet back on the ground, she knew for certain. *This* was where she was meant to be.

Epilogue

Lanterns hung from every post inside the Triple Peak barn. Borrowed tables sat in a line along one side, overflowing with food. And at the back, three fiddlers played an upbeat tune on a makeshift stage. Everywhere Yetta looked, people were having a good time. Some eating, many drinking, and others dancing the two-step in the large open area.

It had been two weeks since the flood, and—with a lot of help—Yetta had managed to organize a huge party. They all had a lot to celebrate.

Practically everyone from Colorado Springs was in attendance, along with everyone from the camp at Nolan Gulch—including Sebastian Carter. Doc Miller was none too pleased about his patient getting out of bed and leaving the boarding house. Let alone to attend a party.

Mrs. Chandler was grateful to have Ava Jones staying at the boarding house. She had been an immense help in nursing Sebastian back to health. In fact, Ava had barely left his side all night.

Yetta thought she detected an attraction between the

two, and that made her so happy. Maybe Sebastian would be the way for Ava to break free of her father.

"You're awful quiet over here," Nathaniel said, sidling up and wrapping an arm around her waist.

Yetta's mouth curled into a smile. She rested her head against Nathaniel's shoulder.

"Just watching everyone enjoying themselves."

"How about you? Are you enjoying yourself?" he asked.

"I couldn't be happier."

"Ooo-wee!" Simpson hooted as he and Clara danced on by, spinning and kicking.

Yetta's smile widened.

Nathaniel held out his hand. "Shall we?"

Yetta put her hand in his, and they joined the line of couples dancing around the room. She let out a giggle when he raised her hand above her head and she spun in a circle under his arm.

This was truly the best night of her life.

Author's Note

I hope you enjoyed reading Yetta's Yearning as much as I did writing it. Do you want to know what's next for Sebastian? Or if Ava will ever break free of her overprotective father? Stay tuned as the Sunsets and Saddles Series continues with Sebastian's Savior.

About the Author

Michele Lindsey lives in upstate New York with her husband, a puppy also known as "Baby Shark," and two kitty overlords. She is the mother of two young adults and has been an ice-cream scooper, a wedding DJ, a balloon-toting clown, a travel agent and a dental assistant.

Currently known in the publishing world as M.L. Stoughton, author of young adult paranormal romance, this is Michele Lindsey's first release for historical western romance. She is a member of RWA (Romance Writers of America) and its local chapter, STAR (Southern Tier Authors of Romance). Her first novel, Pleasantwick, won a gold medal in the 2017 Readers' Favorite Awards and was chosen as the "Official Selection" for Young Adult Fantasy in the 2017 New Apple Summer E-book Awards.

If you want to know more about what she's working on, please visit her website at www.mlstoughton.com or sign up for her email list. http://eepurl.com/b2Qtv5

Also by this Author

Young adult paranormal romance two-book series.

Pleasantwick

Pleasantwick Falling

What's Next for The Alphabet Mail-Order Brides

What's that you say? You're desperately curious what's going on back at the Wigg School and Foundling Home? Is Wiggie pulling her shenanigans with the other teachers? You can find out in Zara's Zephyr

Zara Wigg is a dreamer. So, when she's offered the chance to build her own school and become a mail-order bride, she agrees to all conditions—including the one about taking a husband. But when she arrives in Promise Creek and discovers the man she's fallen in love with through letters isn't her intended, those dreams collapse.

THADDEUS GRAY HAS ONE GOAL: to strike it rich. His sole focus has been on his gold mine, but after writing letters to someone else's bride, life takes a turn. The woman he wrote to is the only one he's ever seen a future with, but any relationship with her is impossible. When her engagement dissolves and she's left in a precarious position, he steps in to help her, regardless of the personal cost.

Yetta's Yearning

. . .

As word gets out of her need for a husband in the woman-hungry town, chaos erupts. Thaddeus is thrown into the position of protector and matchmaker, but as her deadline to marry approaches, he must decide which is more important…love or gold.

Made in the USA
Lexington, KY
20 February 2019